OF VIOLENCE
AND CLICHÉ

ALSO BY M C JOUDREY

FICTION

Etchings in the Dead Wax

Charleswood Road Stories

OF VIOLENCE AND CLICHÉ

M. C. JOUDREY

AT BAY PRESS
WINNIPEG, CANADA

Library and Archives Canada Cataloguing in Publication is available upon request.

ISBN: 978-0-9917610-9-8

Jacket illustration and design by the author.

Set in Fairfield and Century Gothic.

Printed and bound in Canada.

First Paperback Edition January 2016.

Published in Canada by At Bay Press.

Visit At Bay Press's website:
www.atbaypress.com

10 9 8 7 6 5 4 3 2 1

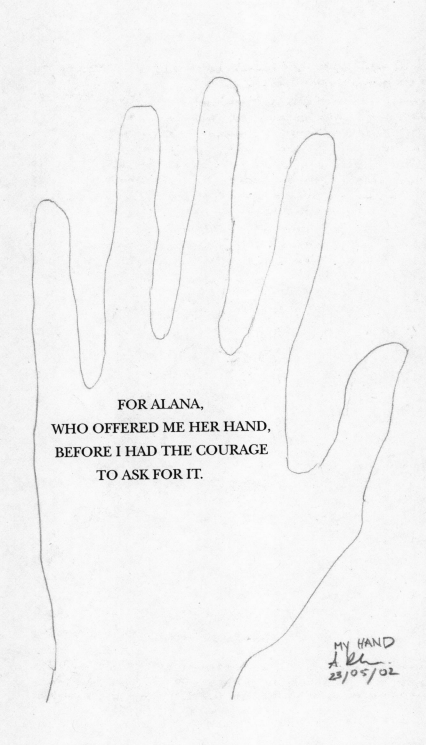

FOR ALANA,
WHO OFFERED ME HER HAND,
BEFORE I HAD THE COURAGE
TO ASK FOR IT.

MY HAND
23/05/02

CHAPTER 1

May 30th 2006

Crows in a nearby poplar were laughing at me, for the hell of it. They cackled, cawed and chuckled like humans tend to do from time to time, when they lay eyes on an unfortunate soul. The best thing about being dead is that these types of things don't get to you anymore. I'm still alive though.

Everything was wet. The air smelled of minerals and the streets were mirror surfaces. The sky above churned as the laminated leaves gathered raindrops. The door was dry; the awning had kept it so. I reached out to tentatively touch it. Curled emerald paint chips broke from the door's surface and fell like wounded butterflies until they lay still on the rotting porch floorboards. The painted flecks sat there only a moment, until the wind carried them off someplace to expire. I started to knock.

"Open up!"

It had been pouring all morning and hadn't let up. I was soaked through to the skin. My bruises ached. My cuts were bloated and burned hot.

My thoughts were jumbled. So much had happened and I was running out of time to figure things out. I put my hands against my temples where I could feel the rhythmic thumping of blood pushing its way through. I massaged my head in attempt to strain the fragments of thought floating in cerebral soup. It didn't help.

It's possible to see enough real life that you'll want to put your eyes out. I ran my hands over my face and then held them out in front if me; they were trembling. Looking at the old door in front of me, my mind started to recede to some other place. I shook my head. Maybe it was the paint chips, or maybe I had taken the wrong blow to the head and my synapses fired strangely at that moment. Maybe I was just really tired or just overexposed and cold from the rain. Maybe I was just finally realizing that human life is just that fragile, even my own.

I knocked again, this time harder.

"Open up, Tracy!"

I heard her footsteps. The latch turned and the door gave way, releasing just a sliver of light. The smell of stale tobacco skulked through the opening and hit my face harder than any knuckles I'd ever taken. She peeked through the crack. I could see the years tattooed on her face. She squinted back at me without recognition in her eyes, but that lasted only a moment until she looked into mine. My eyes were my fingerprints.

"What do you want, William?"

It felt like a lifetime since I had heard her say that name.

"Just a bed for a few hours."

She studied my face. If the apparent scabs and bruising moved her, she did not show it. A cigarette hung loosely from her lips and the ash was in need of attention.

"It's been almost seven years," she said questioningly, but with little enough interest that did not request a response. Then her composure changed and she looked at me hard, her eyes speculative.

"Look, I'm not here for money. I'm just tired, you know? I could use some rest for a little while. I don't need anything else." I shuffled a bit on the doorstep.

She didn't speak. She just looked me over again and opened the door all the way. I took the opportunity and stepped inside.

The place looked the same as my memory of it. Seven years hadn't done much; the carpet looked a little older and the ghost image burned on the television screen was a little more obvious. The aged brown sofa beached in front of it had stains and cigarette burns riddled throughout the upholstery. I reminded myself I didn't look much better.

"You know the way." She motioned with her arm as she sat back down and stubbed out her cigarette on the TV tray beside the sofa. She lit another. Languid smoke still coiled upwards from the dead cigarette.

She didn't look at me and resumed watching whatever was on TV like I wasn't there. She had changed into her Form, a grey raccoon. For as long as I had been able to see these things, I noticed that most people's Forms were grey and hers was no different. Then I caught the smell of them; in the corner of the room, two Shrikun stood motionlessly, poised, as they knew her time was soon and greys had always been easy to convert to black. One of the Shrikun looked at me and smiled, if you could call it that. Raccoons

3

are common animals and common animals always made the best Forms for the Shrikun to acquire. They could be used more often than the more unique animals. They were less conspicuous and therefore more desirable.

I looked back at Tracy, who had reverted to herself again. In the corner, the Shrikun were gone. I made my way upstairs.

I sat on the corner of the bed and pulled off my wet shirt. The diluted stains of blood and grime had mixed into a dark mahogany colour. I hung it on the bedpost to dry and pulled my socks off. The air felt cool against my feet, which had pruned from being wet all morning. I laid the socks on the edge of the old dresser and did the same with my wet jeans and boxer shorts.

I stood up and studied my body for the first time in three days. I had two long cuts, one across my stomach and the other down the middle of my left side. Both weren't deep and had closed. I pulled three small shards of glass from just above my hipbone and set them on the night table. Blood slowly filled the wounds. I had bruising all along my left arm and could feel others along my back. My right thigh had also sustained a cut, although I couldn't remember the source. As I mentioned, so much had happened.

There was a small mirror on the dresser, and I picked it up to look at my face. I didn't look good; it wasn't just that I hadn't slept in three days, it was worse. I set the mirror down and sat back on the edge of the bed. The clock on the night table told me it was mid-afternoon.

I opened my eyes again at four in the morning. I didn't remember lying down and my body ached as I sat up. The room was dark. The sun had quit and the moon had forgotten to show up for its shift.

I made fists with my hands a couple of times. I stood up and reached for my shirt. It had dried and smelled foul. As I pulled it over my head, I realized the sleep hadn't helped much with the pain, but then I hadn't expected a miracle. Still, my head was clear and that was the thing that mattered most. My socks had coiled awkwardly as they dried, and felt abrasive as I pulled them over my feet. My jeans were still completely damp.

I went to the washroom and took a piss. I spat in the sink and turned on the water, running my hands underneath the faucet. I cupped my hands to splash a little water on my face and ran my cold wet hand over the back of my neck. There wasn't much in the rusty medicine cabinet; a tube of old toothpaste and some bandages (which I used) were the only indications of personal hygiene. There were also a few loose razorblades and I picked one up and checked the blade edge with my fingertip. It was still sharp. I pocketed the metallic rectangle as I knew it would work perfectly.

Coming down the steps, I saw Tracy was still watching the television and it didn't look like she had moved at all since earlier that afternoon. Did she not sleep anymore? I stopped a moment and looked around again. I could feel my past life crawling like cockroaches behind the old manila-coloured walls.

I slipped on my shoes and went for the door. As Tracy got up from her chair, I quickly tied my laces, then stood up and looked at her standing in front of me. A part of me wanted her to say something. She didn't.

"Thanks," I offered.

Her face stiffened when I said it, but then softened, surprisingly. I hadn't said it in a long time, not to her, not to anyone. She knew this was the last time she would see me and looked me in the eyes. She then turned away and headed towards the kitchen. And that was that. I opened the door and left.

Out on the porch, the temperature had warmed and the early morning air was stagnant and humid. The rain had stopped but everything was still wet and heavy. My stomach barked at me. Just another thing, I thought, staring out into the foggy dawn. Outside, there were no sounds at all and for a moment, I knew peace. Then I heard the door open behind me. I turned around and Tracy was standing there in the doorway.

"Open your hand, William," she said softly.

I did as I was told and my mother handed me an apple.

CHAPTER 2

1994 -
The City
Lamia

Lamia came to me for the first time that year, back when the waterfront was still innocent. You could see the Dome from the harbour and they still called it the Dome, before Ted felt the need to spray-paint his bloody namesake on it while the mayor sat back and let him do it. The nest was never quite the same after that, but we owned the game in '93. We'll always have that.

The first of the condominiums grew up like dandelions and the gentle breeze off the lake blew the foul seeds of greed into the fertile ground below. The rest of the concrete weeds would soon break the soil and ejaculate forth, robbing everyone of the view of that once great lake, which was now nothing more than alkaline sewage and dead sand.

But before all this, Toronto still answered to its inhabitants and the inhabitants could still feel their city breathing. She pumped life into all those who believed she was the greatest city in the world.

Steel rockets barreled freely beneath the earth. The tower was just the tower, and didn't need lights running up and down its shaft to make it more favorable to its audience. If you listened closely, you could hear it whisper, "Fuck the tourist."

Queen Street West still had its pride, with a myriad of little shops and storefronts, and underground purveyors of the strange and weird. It was a home to the fringe, and there were enough characters to gobble it up completely.

The one thing that still remains the same is that The Horseshoe puts bands that matter on its stage. Everything else has vanished. Today, Queen Street West is merely a bargain version of Rodeo Drive, filled with big box American fashion stores raping the last of our Canadian cool. We should have all shouted that horrible "C" word at them from a megaphone; rubbing in the dirty, degrading little word that only the most morally-amputated individuals say with pleasure, right into their greedy faces. We should have tattooed it right on their foreheads where it belongs in bold black letters: Capitalist.

There should've been a revolution. But there wasn't and all of us are to blame. We let them have it and didn't even raise an eyebrow. Today we support them like they were that dealer with the really good stuff. We pay them to advertise their brand's name on our chests and we walk around as a congregation of happy human billboards.

The Gardiner heralded the suburbanites forth into a majestic metropolitan core every morning. At night, as the gleaming sentinels grew smaller in their rear views, they would lie to themselves, somewhat convinced that they were better off in the suburbs. They knew better though; deep down they knew the city was the heart and suburbs were cardiac arrests disguised as strip malls.

Streetcars ground along the King Street tracks; up through Chinatown and the "Littles", like Italy, Portugal, and India, they carried passengers like veins carry white blood cells towards the source of infection.

The Leafs were a good team; no one remembers that, but they were, and Joes and Janes could afford to attend the games. The Gardens, God rest its beautiful soul, stands alone and forgotten today like an antiquated Chinese daughter, but back then it housed the kind of patron our great game deserved. Now the Suits own the whole first section, leaving nothing but vacancy in a centre named for some tired, tainted aviation corporation, bailed out far too many times to be worth naming here.

I lived in this city. I loved this city, my city, my Toronto. Every pulse and pump pushed me into the next minute with fervour. I moved with the madness and was laid down to sleep by the fluorescent glow of the city lights at night. There was a truth to it. I couldn't ask for more and didn't want for anything. I had everything I needed, and that's a life worth living.

Things were good. That's a word people use too often to describe just about everything. Truth is, my life was good in the true definition of the word. Good like content, good like loved, good like healthy, good like having purpose. Maybe if things had kept on that way, I don't know, it could've all been different. But chance doesn't work like that.

I was 22 that year when she just appeared in front of me. Well, there was more to it than that. There was the accident. I don't remember much. I was hurt pretty bad. I couldn't move my legs. They were pinned under me. I remember the left side of my head was itchy so I touched it. It was warm and wet, and when I took my hand away and it was stained crimson. There was an awful smell and a lot of smoke. I must have blacked out for a minute or so.

I was sleeping, or at least it felt like I was asleep, because someone shook me awake. You know that feeling when you're at the edge between sleep and waking? You want to stay in the realm of rest but something is tugging at you, trying to bring you back into wakefulness. That's what it was like.

When I came to, I fought a valiant war with my heavy eyelids and won. There were flames in front of me and they were rapidly getting closer.

"You should get out of there."

The voice was sweet and soft. It was female. I looked for its origin.

"I'm over here, silly. Look left."

I did as I was told. It was an angel.

"I'm not an angel."

"Do you know my thoughts?"

"No, but I've dealt with your kind before. You all think the same thing the first time."

She wore a billowing blue silk skirt that caught the firelight, and the steady breeze folded the seemingly endless loose fabric like waves lapping at the beach. On her waist sat a golden snakeskin belt, but her torso was completely bare and her skin luminescent. Her body was gloriously feminine, with long cascading red hair that glowed like Jason's fleece, hanging obediently at her back. She appeared human but was far too beautiful to be anything but a deity

10

of some kind. She looked at me and then lowered her eyes, and I followed their gaze.

"Don't stare at my tits!"

I was, and she scolded me in a malicious yet playful manner as though she had tricked me into doing it.

"Who are you?"

"I don't think that's important right now, do you?"

I surveyed my surroundings and realized that in only a matter of moments I would be consumed by flames.

"Can you help me? I'm stuck."

"I can't, not like that."

"Why not?"

I had become angry almost instantly.

"Anger is good. You'll need a lot of it. Now if you had given me a chance, I would have explained to you that I couldn't physically help you. I can cheer you on though."

"You're mocking me?"

" A little, yes." She smiled at me.

"Why? Why won't you help me?"

"As I said, I can't." She was nonchalantly inspecting her fingernails.

I became incensed. Rage overtook me, fueled by her callous indifference to my situation. The flames came closer and I struggled to free my legs. I pushed with everything I had and then I gave up, my legs wedged in, tight as ever.

"Are you a screamer? I mean, when you start to burn and all. Do you think you'll wail and moan like a child?"

"Why are you doing this?"

"Me? You did this, remember? I wasn't driving, feeling all sorry for myself. Tsk, never drive under the influence of depression."

She smiled at me again. She was enjoying this. I felt my blood boil beneath my skin. I reached forward and pulled at the moulding on the dash that had been forced in on my legs. It wouldn't budge. I lost control and started to rain my fists upon it, hitting it until my knuckles bled. The large piece of moulding came completely free, and I pulled my left leg out. My jeans had a series of long cuts that ran up the shin and blood had soaked them thoroughly, but having the extra space now allowed room for me to get my right leg free.

The flames began to engulf the entire area, surrounding me, chewing voraciously through my clothes. I could smell my own flesh burning. I rolled in pain from the automobile into the dirt, and batted at the stubborn flames on my shirt-sleeves. I could hear the woman's laughter as I fumbled on the ground.

I fought my way to my feet despite the searing pain in my shins. I felt my anger hemorrhage into fury, and I reached out with my bloody hands, put them around her throat and squeezed with ardent pleasure. She laughed only harder at me. I tightened my grip but it had no effect. She stopped laughing and looked into my eyes.

"I'm going to like spending time with you, Willie."

I released my grip.

"Do you know who I am?" I asked, my rage subsiding.

"I do." She looked at me laconically. Her eyes wandered back towards the car, which was now a red and yellow inferno. A rogue flame found the fuel line, and within seconds the vehicle exploded. In my blind fury and confusion, I had not distanced myself enough from the blast. I was thrown off my feet and hit the asphalt with a wicked force. Again, it was lights out.

CHAPTER 3

Maneki

I woke in the hospital. Mine was the only bed in the room. A doctor and nurse were standing next to my bed, quietly talking to each other when the transformations happened; the doctor changed in front of me and became a grey-coloured bear and the nurse a white sheep. I blinked my eyes hard and they looked like normal people again. Maybe I wasn't in a hospital after all.

"Where am I?"

They turned to face me and were both smiling. The doctor spoke.

"You're at St. Michael's and you were in a car accident. Do you remember that?"

"I remember."

"You're very lucky to be alive. You've sustained quite a blow to the head. We've done a number of tests and so far everything looks fine. There were also a number of minor lacerations and some bruising, but you should recover with some rest."

"How long have I been out?"

"Most of the day. You were brought in last night."

"What time is it?"

"Nine pm. There's a clock on the wall just over there."

"How long do I have to stay here?"

"Another night, maybe two. We try to monitor accident cases closely, especially when there's any head trauma. In the meantime, just push that button beside your bed if you need anything."

"Thanks."

"You're welcome."

The doctor left the room and the nurse changed my empty saline pouch.

"I'll be right back with some water."

And then I was alone. I was tired and my head throbbed but I was in a lot less pain than I had expected. I suspect it wasn't just saline I was getting through my IV.

I had trouble keeping my eyes open. I tried to wait for my water. But the white veil was too much for me. I woke almost two hours later. There was a glass of water on the table beside me. I reached for it and took a drink, but it did nothing but add to the cotton film that had covered the roof of my mouth. I set the plastic cup back on the table.

At the foot of my bed sat an orange tabby cat, looking at me with his tail playfully curling at one side. It was strange; I hadn't felt him jump up onto my bed, nor did I even feel him sitting there. We stared at each other for a moment. The colours of his face remained sharp and the proportions accurate. This vision wasn't due to the morphine. The fuzzy little quadruped was almost certainly real.

"What's your name, fur ball?"

"Maneki, and don't call me fur ball."

I recoiled in terror, pulling my feet up as close to me as possible, away from the creature. Maybe the morphine hadn't fully run its course.

"You know, there was a time when I was naive enough to think human reaction to something hardly fathomable wouldn't get old. You know what I mean? I say boo, and your skeleton bursts from your skin or some such nonsense. Millennia have come and gone, and it's safe to say it's getting old."

"What are you?"

"A cat. Wow, for once Lamia wasn't lying. You really did hit your head."

"I must be going crazy."

I said it out loud like the words would smother the vibrant orange creature and the power of admission would just make it disappear. It didn't.

"Don't do that."

"What?"

"The whole 'I'm going crazy' bit, because you see and hear a talking cat. It belittles us both."

"I don't understand."

"Okay, now that I can help you with."

I threw my hands up in the air.

"I'm all ears!"

"No you're not. Why do humans always use exaggerated idioms?"

I just stared blankly at the creature, not even hearing the question. I could feel a large group of words trapped in my throat like a wad of over-spooned baby food, but could not find a way to spit them up.

"Never mind. Look pal, I'm here simply because you hit your head. If you listen closely I should be able to provide some insight on what's going on here, get it?"

I nodded. It's what you do in situations like these. I fidgeted in my bed and sat upright as best I could, despite the pain. I did this partly to get a better look at the cat, but more importantly to gain a little distance from it.

"I'm a Neko. Apparently it was a Japanese chick that was the first to see one of us a few thousand years ago. Hence the term Neko, which actually just means luck."

The cat looked at me inquisitively to see if its words were registering in any way. It made absolutely no sense at all, but I nodded halfheartedly, hoping he'd continue.

"As I mentioned, my name is Maneki. It is a real pleasure to meet you, William."

"You know my name? The woman from last night knew me too."

"That was Lamia, she's a daemon and a real piece of work. We know your name and most of your life's history. What I can't tell you is why this is happening to you. We aren't given that information. There are very few people like you who can see us, and we are not quite sure why this is the case. It's not like you've been chosen for some quest to save the world and even if that were true, the powers that be would never tell me so, let alone that wacko Lamia. What's even rarer is when someone starts to see us later in life, like you can, due to a bump on the head."

I reached up and felt the bandages around my head.

"That's right bucko, you hit your head and that has caused your synapses to register certain things in different ways. This has happened only a handful of times before in thousands of years, to my recollection."

"I hope I don't get the pleasure of meeting more of your kind."

"Actually, we are very few. We're not always cats, but usually a creature that has a naturally good rapport with people and are numerous and common, like squirrels or crows. We get assigned to a person and we're with them for the rest of their life, be it a long one or a short one. I don't know why, I just know I am supposed to provide you with ongoing information and stay close in order to help in some way. Truth is I don't really bring luck. I just do my best to be helpful."

The cat tilted his head to one side, trying to discern the expression on my face. It licked one of its forepaws and then continued to yammer on.

"The last guy I was assigned to was a serial killer. You might imagine it was an exciting assignment. He wasn't much for conversation, though."

The cat looked out absently into the hallway.

"You can't ask me direct questions about the things you're going to see." Maneki was waiting for me to say something. I didn't though.

"If you do ask me direct questions about what's really out there, well, I can't answer them, nor can I speak about them ever again. It's natural to want to ask, as humans are curious to a fault. But you can't. You have to wait for me to tell you about it and you can't ask me to elaborate on the things I've told you either."

"Seems stupid."

"Joke if you want to. These are the hard and fast rules."

All this talk about rules jogged my memory to what the strange woman had said to me when I was trapped in the car.

"The half-naked woman, Lamia, she refused to help me last night."

I was about to formulate a question, but stopped myself before I did.

"Well done, William. You have learned your first and most valuable lesson in this new game of ours. You may talk idly about the things you want to know but if you phrase it in the form of a question, well, no point in being repetitive. However, you can ask me questions about unrelated or seemingly unrelated topics." I nodded, trying to absorb the crazy details.

"Unfortunately, Lamia is mostly an enigma to me. I do know she is the only one of her kind and she can help you in ways that I can't, if she will help you at all."

The cat began to stretch his two front legs out in front of himself.

"These late nights are killing me."

My head was throbbing. I remembered how the nurse and doctor had looked like animals when I had first come around. I chuckled out loud at the complete absurdity and the apparent state of my sanity.

"What's so funny?"

"Sorry, I was just thinking about how when I woke up tonight the nurse looked like a sheep and the doctor like a bear. I could see their animal mouths moving as they talked."

The cat looked at me solidly.

"What colour were they?"

The smile left my face.

"The bear, I mean the doctor was grey and the nurse was white."

The cat looked down at his paws.

"You've seen their Forms. This is rare, especially for unnatural viewers such as you. Humans don't usually start to see Forms for many months, sometimes even years. Every human being has a Form; it is the true nature of their soul. Each Form appears as white, black, or grey. White Forms are souls that are intact, honest and pure. Their intentions are without malice and their morals are secure. Black Forms are corrupt and are the antithesis of white Forms. Greys are complicated and are either mostly pure or mostly corrupt and seldom equal on both accounts. Sadly, grey souls are turned black more often than not."

"Can a black Form ever become white again?"

"William, we went over this. If you ask me a direct question I can never answer it."

"Not ever?"

"No, not ever."

The cat yawned, curled up and closed its eyes at the foot of my bed.

"Get some sleep, William."

I was aghast at the futility of my situation. I lay there thinking and watching the sleeping cat. The doctor came down the hallway and into the room. He checked the machines behind me.

"How are you feeling?"

"Tired. My head hurts."

"Get some rest. You'll feel better in the morning."

The doctor turned and started to leave the room. I looked down at the cat that was in a deep sleep at my feet.

"Oh doctor, that cat isn't mine."

The doctor scanned the room, and then he looked at me with a very concerned and furrowed brow.

"What cat?"

CHAPTER 4

1997 –
The Louse

If I looked a little foolish it was because I was wearing a foolish smile. In real life, no man sports a smile when he's outnumbered. It's only in the movies that the hero smiles as he's about to get his ass kicked.

I had met Loudon the Louse two nights ago in a bar. He was a small fish in a big pond of crooks. Still, he was connected to some true fellas and I figured if I landed some kind of gig with him I could work my way up, just like the swine on Bay Street.

Loudon had invited me to a meeting, which turned out to be a street fight where I was outnumbered two to one. That's why they call him the Louse. That's also why I was sporting the smile I was, whereas other guys would be emptying their bowels into their Calvins. I'm a fighter and a good one, but these guys didn't know it yet. My smile un-settled them.

"Boy must be retarded or something, just stands there smiling. You ever see something like this before, Reggie?"

"Never, man, never. Kid must be retarded."

"You retarded our something, kid? I mean, you know what this is, right? You know where you are? This isn't the schoolyard; you're in some serious shit here. Ain't that right, Reggie?"

"Serious shit!"

"We gonna hand you your balls, boy."

"Juan, show him your toy, maybe that'll clean the smile off his face."

Only cowards talk like this and we all know the world is full of cowards. Some like to chirp when they fight. They think it gives them an edge, puts a little fear in their oppo-nent. Sometimes that's true, if your opponent is just some guy who has never fought a real fight before. I knew my stupid smile was getting to them and the less I said the more they showed their weaknesses. The best fighters were always those who used basic psychology as an opener and followed through with their knuckles.

Juan took out a six-inch folding knife with serrated teeth on the backside of the steel; a mean little instrument that he bent open to lock the blade into place. It didn't change anything. Reggie was still my target. In a bold move, I ad-vanced first and watched Juan step back a little. I expected this; he was the smarter of the two and let Reggie open. They might have had a chance if they came at me togeth-er, but people don't think like that. Their egos make them think only of themselves. They want to win alone or stay safe alone.

Reggie moved a bit better than I had initially anticipated. I caught a glimmer of his Form, a black fox. He reverted instantly back and almost connected with an admirable right cross, but his posture and positioning were poor, which left me a wide-open window to his Adam's apple. I made good with a wrecking ball blow that finished him.

It was just Juan and I now. His Form was boldly revealed to me as a black raccoon. I moved to him, which startled him only slightly. He couldn't run, because he knew what the end result of that would be with Loudon, so he put the blade out in front of him for protection. I've seen a handful of knife fights and Juan wouldn't fare well. He held the knife too tightly, which slows your timing if you need to shift the grip position on the handle. He also had extended his arm out in front of him, until his elbow was locked. He had no room left to thrust the blade and all I had to do was be a little creative with my footwork. I got past his knife hand and put a fist in his gut. He doubled over, bringing his arms and the knife in close to his chest. I kicked the blade out of his hand, and sent a pile driver fist into the back of his neck. I felt his vertebrae break beneath his skin with a muted cracking sound. A barely audible noise escaped Juan's throat and he was dead before he met the dirt.

I went over and scooped up the knife lying amongst some gravel, and made my way towards Loudon. I would have my revenge.

"Be at the Cottonmouth Pool Hall on College tomorrow at noon."

The confidence in his voice abruptly halted my advance. I looked down at my chest and a glowing red dot hovered over my sternum like a common housefly. The louse had come prepared. This was an interview, and I got the job.

The Louse drove away and I stood in silence, dumb-founded. I had been outsmarted and it was only by virtue of luck and skill that I had come out ahead. This wasn't like Bay Street at all—you didn't risk getting fired or losing your pride, you risked losing your life, or worse.

A strange sound came from behind me and I turned quickly, holding the knife out in front of me. What I saw before me shook me to the very core of my being. I dropped the knife and took two slow steps backwards. It was the only time I ever backed away in my life.

In front of me was a creature that stood like a human but looked animalistic, wolfish almost. Its eyes were cavernous yet penetrating and it made a rasping sound that quickened my blood. It was standing over Juan's dead body, which had reverted to its raccoon Form.

The creature looked up like it was inspecting me and then down at Juan. The creature's hideous mouth opened wide and it began to inhale the very essence of Juan's Form, swallowing it like fresh oxygen to the lungs. When it had absorbed all of Juan's Form, it looked back down at the empty shell that was once his humanity.

A guttural sound came from behind the creature and then a muffled curse. A wino was lying against the wall of the alley, drinking from his bottle. I had looked away only momentarily and then back at the creature. It had turned into a raccoon Form, similar to Juan's former existence, and was well on its way towards the drunk. I caught a glimpse of the drunk's Form, a grey hound dog. The raccoon approached the man as he took a swig from his bottle, and bit him in the arm.

"Fuckin' brazen 'coons! Damn things is everywhere in this city." He threw an empty bottle at the animal but missed. The creature scurried behind a dumpster.

I looked at the drunk and his Form had turned from grey to black.

"That's what they do."

I looked down and Maneki was circling my feet.

"What are you doing here?"

"You're getting better at your questions. You know why I'm here." I'll never get used to it; it will always be strange when that cat smiles at me.

"Yeah well, you learn quick when you want to know about something crazy, like what I just witnessed."

"Right, about that. You just saw your first Shrikun." Maneki looked up at me and waited. He was stalling to see if I'd ask the obvious question, which would stop him from ever being able to tell me what a Shrikun, or whatever he called it, was. Then I'd have to try to get it out of Lamia, and that was almost always a fruitless endeavour.

"Good lad."

I smiled.

"Shrikun appear when someone dies or is about to die. They are collectors, takers of human Forms. They can actually only take black Forms. Once a Shrikun takes a Form, they can transform into whatever Form they have acquired. You saw a black raccoon die and the Shrikun took the Form for its own use."

"Ugh, there is no end to this crap, Maneki."

The orange tabby looked at me, stone-faced.

"No, not until you die anyway."

"What about me, why can't I see my own Form?"

"I can't answer that. Not now or ever."

"Damn!"

"You know better than to do that."

"I know, I know. These goddamn rules!"

I took a deep breath and ran my hands through my hair. I cursed again under my breath and then made eye contact with the cat.

"Stop cursing, William."

"Don't tell me what to do!"

The cat licked his fur carelessly, like an adult pretending to have infinite patience for a misbehaving child.

"Do you want to hear more about the Shrikun, or shall we call it a night?"

I kicked an empty bottle, the last childish outburst I allowed myself before I got it together.

"Go on."

"Shrikun use Forms against people to manipulate them or trick them."

The damn cat paused again. I said nothing and he smiled at me.

"Humans mostly trust animals. Shrikun use that trust against people. They are clever creatures. Their goal is to convert whites to greys and then finally greys to blacks. A Form that dies grey becomes nothing. It just vanishes and is a loss to the Shrikun."

"It just vanishes?"

The cat looked at me speculatively and I realized I messed up again.

"Reiteration is allowed. The truth is, I don't know for sure what happens to greys. Lamia might know. I do know that whites go somewhere, that I am sure of, but I don't know where or what the place might be. It's beyond my clearance, so to speak."

The cat stopped with its explanation and looked up at me.

"What's this I hear about you going by another name? Kent or something?"

"I'm assuming Lamia told you that? Not sure how she'd even know about it."

"It's her business to know things about you."

"Social norms haven't ever mattered all that much to me. I never liked William and I can call myself whatever I want."

"That is true, but neither I or Lamia can. Whatever name is on your birth certificate is the name we must address you by."

"Why?"

"Oh William. Rules are rules."

"Bunch of crap, that's all that is."

Without warning, the cat broke from beside my feet and ran into the shadows. There was the sound of an overturned garbage can and then silence. I watched the shadows for a moment, and then the tabby emerged with something hanging from between its teeth. I looked closely and realized it was a mouse that he had just captured and killed.

"Don't give me that look." Maneki swallowed the dead rodent whole and then licked his paws. "After all, I am still a cat."

CHAPTER 5

1999 –
Spilled Milk

Me, I'm not one of the good ones. I want to get this out of the way right now before there are any misunderstandings. I'm the nick when you shave, the skip in the record.

I don't lie to myself like the Italians do by trying to fit in. Goddamn Mafia, there's some expired fruit if I ever saw any. Heck, most people lie to themselves more than they tell themselves the truth. Life is easier that way. That's why so many people believe in God, to have a reason for their struggle.

Imagine being content working for some manager who clock watches the shit out of your shift. There's nothing more dangerous than a person who believes to their core in the ideals of a faceless corporation. More output is expected from you each year despite recessions and market crashes. Toil away for two weeks off out of 52. Pay bills, taxes to a government that embezzles it for whores and heart surgeries. Routine is a clever way of saying suicide, just depends on the scale you're using to measure these things.

We're the chosen beasts, the animal burdened with self-awareness. No child tells their parent that when they grow up they want to take inventory, clean toilets, or sell insurance. What if we lived in a world where people didn't give up on their dreams, had hope, and saw things through to the end? People don't understand that their dreams are as important as eating and breathing. Most of us don't even ask why it takes us so long to fall asleep at night or the reason for those headaches. That's most people. Me, I'd rather put my fist into another man's milky throat and fly through life anonymously any day. Maybe I've navigated my way through the complexities of the simple 24-hour heart-beat or maybe I'm just simple, you do the math.

I didn't work for Loudon for very long. About two years, give or take a few months. In those days, the Louse had a pool hall off College Street that isn't there anymore, much like the rest of College Street that I used to know. I worked for him for about a year, taking book and roughing up jacks that owed him money. I didn't like the work, but I got to meet the kind of people who could help me get ahead and sometimes I'd come into a sizable stack of cabbage. Loud-on was bad at keeping tabs on his staff and in turn, missed a lot of side transactions. That's what happens when you fill your nose with blow three or four times a day. It also made him unpredictable, like most honest-to-badness addicts.

Despite my disdain for the modern working man, I too was in this thing for the scratch. I wanted money and more importantly, I was encumbered with the same problem every other living chap is faced with, and that problem was very simple: as much as I wanted money, I needed it even more. So yeah, I'm a hypocrite. Show me someone breathing who isn't.

Loudon was a real poison peach though, and was unpredictable at best. Unstable people can't be trusted. They tip the scales in favour of chaos, although a little chaos at the right time is good, in my humble opinion. Keeps us all honest. But the Louse, well, he was different. He had a temper too.

Loudon would beat up on this immigrant kid with a gimp arm who used to come to the hall from time to time. Once, he decided to lay into the kid and give him a good going over. I stepped in before he spread on the icing, and popped Loudon one right in the nose. He lost his footing and tumbled backwards, falling into a cue rack. The cues went all over the floor like an emptied box of toothpicks. He frantically tossed the cues off himself and got up quickly, red in the face with a mark on the snout and nothing much to cry about but boy did he sing.

"You hit me!" He said it as though it hadn't happened yet.

"I did."

"Over this piece of retard shit?" It really was a question he wanted an answer to.

You see Lousy hated the kid because he was a gimp, because he came from another country and he beat up on him for those reasons alone. Not because the kid stole from him, not because the kid irritated him, but because he was brown and handicapped to boot. So I let him know what it felt like to be the smaller of two people. I never much liked bullies. It gave me great pleasure to set one right on his ass.

"You should leave the kid be, Lou." I wasn't asking and he knew it.

"You should know your place." He didn't deliver his words with confidence and everyone in the place was now watching. He knew that, too.

"I've got to go make some calls."

I turned my back to him and started to walk away

"Now hold on a second, I ain't finished talking to you yet."

"No, we're done here."

I kept on walking. Loudon put foot to floor and came after me, gripped my arm, spun me around and lunged forth with a telegraphed roundhouse. I moved and he missed. Then I put a cowbell fist into his left cheek that sent him round like a dreidel. He was done and so was my time in his employ.

I learned something very valuable about the industry I was entering into. This thing, this street game of players and pawns has eyes and those eyes are always on the lookout for fresh meat. I didn't know it at the time, but that little play didn't go unnoticed and it landed me an interview for another job.

It's my belief that every single person was born to be really great at something. Maybe it's painting or baseball. Maybe it's cooking or killing. Everyone has a skill inside that is well hidden, waiting to be discovered and put into play. Most people never get to know what it is they were born to do. I was about to get that chance.

CHAPTER 6

Arnie

We are all of us human, some just a little less so than others. I watched the guy to the left of me rain heaps of salt upon his French fries. He said his name was Rusty. The Polack on my right didn't speak any English, had weak eyes, stunk wretchedly of mothballs, and I was pretty sure he could carry himself in a tussle.

The Polack, who went by Stentinowski, stared with disgust as Rusty licked the salt granules off a fry with tedious concentration and put the limp golden rod back on the serving tray. He did this one by one, treating each side of the rectangular fry with the careful attention of his sweaty tongue. Between each one he'd suck hard on the straw of his pop can, wetting his licker for the next go round.

I had been sandwiched between these two lovelies for about a half an hour, waiting for a guy named Arnie.

Ten minutes later, the face of a criminal strolled into the restaurant with crooked lips and a smile parting them. Arnie wasn't impressive to look at but had killed over a dozen men, raped as many women and couldn't remember the names of any of them. Albanians never do. He had thinning hair slicked and combed towards the back with pride, as you'd imagine a crook would keep his hair. He wore clothes that exceeded his standing in life by satirical margins. All in all, Arnie was a prize, and right there is where I misjudged him. You see, Arnie wore the mask of a fool but underneath was a deadly rattlesnake contorted into the shape of a man. He was cunning and had a willingness to act on desires most folks only read about in their morning newspaper.

Arnie could shed his skin in mere seconds. He was so charming he could talk Joan of Arc into shaking hands with the English and then shrewd enough to convince her it might be nice to have a campfire and celebrate. He was evil; there's an interesting one for ya, but he was the very definition of the word. Arnie couldn't find Jesus in church, but that doesn't carry very far because I could never find him there either.

He placed an order with the fat waiter and a plate of greasy Chink food arrived promptly in front of his greedy mouth. He surveyed the food and put a fork up in my direction.

"You gonna eat?"

"Me?"

"Yeah you, stupid. When I point at you I don't mean the runny yolk next to you."

"I'm not hungry," I said casually.

"I didn't ask if you were hungry, I asked if you are going to eat."

"No."

"No, what?"

"No, I am not going to eat."

"Shit boy, you're going to have a hard life if you can't answer simple directs like the one I just gave you." He smiled at me, slurping back some noodles as he said it. Sauce leaked from the corners of his mouth, traveled downward until it pooled into a droplet beneath his chin and hung there, vibrating precariously for a moment until it came free and fell back onto his plate of food.

Gen Go Chow, only place with a whole bunch of slants running around like free-range chickens serving every kind of food under the sun. They even served burritos. Imagine that, zips serving cholo food. Model minority achievement is happening in this glorious modern North America, right under the belly of the white sloth. The Bible says the meek shall inherit the earth; whoever wrote that hadn't counted on the Chinese work ethic.

Arnie liked the place because the owner usually sent him home with a young girl after the meal. The young girl usually didn't come back the way she left.

"What's your problem?"

Arnie put his fork up in Stentinowski's face. Stentinowski didn't answer because Stentinowski didn't understand Arnie's question. He didn't understand the question because as I said before he didn't speak English. Arnie knew this but asked anyway, because Arnie was a real-life son of a bitch.

With his eyes on his noodles, he looked at me again with his fork. "You know what his problem is?" he asked me, moving his fork back towards Stentinowski.

"I don't."

"I do." He paused as he shoveled another mouthful of white wormy noodles into his gape. He chewed with his mouth open and the noodles churned like real worms all bunched up in a fisherman's bait container.

Stentinowski's eyes bulged at him with a dumbfounded look, while Arnie continued to fork at him.

"You want to preserve your youth. Amen, don't we all! You look preserved, and you sure as hell smell preserved, 'cause all I smell over my food is the awful stink of moth-balls." He looked up from his food at the three of us, like Stentinowski's smell was a group fault.

Stentinowski looked to Rusty and me for help. Then Arnie reached over and slapped him in the face. Hard, but not really hard and nothing that would cause Stentinowski any real pain. Stentinowski's face went childlike, as though his own father had just hit him and he might start to cry. There's nothing more defeating than watching a simple act of violence reduce a man into a state worthy of your pity. I felt nothing for him.

Arnie mindlessly tortured the last noodle on his plate with his fork. I watched him cut it into tiny sections. All he needed now was a magnifying glass and a little bit of sunshine. He looked up from his plate and at me, but addressed the three of us.

"Have you all been introduced?"

We nodded that we had.

"Good. Do you know why you're here?"

There was a long pause and then I spoke up.

"For a job."

"Is that what you were told?"

We nodded in unison again.

"Well it ain't like that. I mean, I brought you in to fight."

We all took an investigative glance at each other.

"Every second Friday I run private, unsanctioned fights in a section near the harbour. You three are on my bill for tonight. You'll fight anywhere from one to three fights, depending on how you do. There's money in it, if you win. If you lose, I don't see you again. Make sense?"

It did and we said so. Arnie looked the three of us over closely.

"Do you have any questions?"

We didn't

"Perfect."

He put a finger in Stentinowski's face.

"Get mean, boy! You won't be able to stink these guys to death!"

Stentinowski had no idea what Arnie said but understood perfectly what he meant from the expression on his face.

Arnie stood up from the table, threw some cash down onto his filthy plate and smiled as the bills mixed with the leftover sauce.

"I will be there at some point tonight. Don't disappoint me, boys."

Seconds later, the manager was standing beside him with an awkward young Chinese waif not even close to legal age. She looked sickly and thin, and there were tracks all up and down her arms. It was her eyes that killed you though; they were grey and lifeless, swimming in rancid morphine. She stood there just looking off into nowhere with her glassy eyes and skin peppered with ripe bruises, like some sort of Asian trout. Arnie put his hands on her waist and gripped her firmly. He looked at her in such a way that a chill rippled through the three of us simultaneously.

He took her by the arm and she apathetically allowed herself to be towed from the restaurant. I watched the limp, lifeless girl vanish through the restaurant doors with evil in its purest form: Man.

CHAPTER 7

Pink
Dark Agnes

The eastern Toronto harbour was quiet at night. It was the commercial section of the harbourfront and therefore received little to no traffic in the evenings and into the night. I hadn't been standing alone long when a man walked out from behind a boathouse and made his way towards me.

"You Kendall?"

"Yep."

"Follow me, please."

I did. The man's accent was thick and I put it somewhere around Eastern Europe, Czech maybe. We walked for ten minutes in silence. I kept looking for some sort of warehouse or factory, but there wasn't much along the wharf that matched the description I had formulated in my mind as to what Arnie's place might look like. Then the man stopped walking and pointed.

"There, you see?"

I nodded that I did.

"You go. Ask for Pink, yeah?"

"Yeah, okay."

The man walked away and was out of view before I managed to collect myself. I headed towards the cruise ship he had pointed to.

The cruise liner was old and nothing that would meet today's standards for fantasy holidays. Still, it was in good seaworthy shape from what I could tell, based on my limited understanding of such things. The name that adorned the boat was "Dark Agnes", which meant nothing to me and the letters were barely visible. It was lightless on the pier and the vessel was moored discretely and purposefully. The ship itself showed no signs of life aboard. If another ship were to pass Dark Agnes on the open water at night, a seafarer would surely think it a ghost ship, or miss it entirely.

I arrived at the base of the gangplank when a man appeared. He was older, maybe in his fifties, with a head full of grey hair that was kept neat and short. His face was a little too meaty but didn't detract from his overall ruggedly handsome appearance. He was smoking a cigarette and he took a pull on the filter. He wore a white collared shirt with the top two buttons flying loose, exposing a portion of grey chest hair. His sleeves were rolled up comfortably as the night temperature was warm. He carried himself with an insouciant air that belied his true characteristics. He looked down at me and then spoke.

"Nice night."

"If you're into that."

He smiled a little at my reply.

"You Kendall?"

This man also had a similar accent, but it was subtle.

"Yes. You Pink?"

"Pinkerton, but some call me Pink and a few have said Pinky." He paused and reflected a moment like he was going to add something more, but then didn't.

"Uh huh, whatever."

"You're late."

"No, I'm not."

"You calling me a liar?"

"Yes."

"Well, I am lying. First time in my life. I just like to check a fighter's spirit so as not to waste anyone's time." He laughed. It was a good laugh and he shifted to his Form momentarily. It was black tiger.

"Do I come up or not?"

"Come, come!"

I mounted the gangplank and made my way aboard. When I reached the top of the plank, the man named Pink threw his arm around my shoulders as he guided me indoors.

"Where were you born?"

"Here."

"Toronto?"

"Uh huh."

"You a popular boy? Got a lot of chums?"

"Nope."

He looked at me suspiciously.

"No friends?"

"Nope, not much of a people person."

He laughed.

41

"This I can tell." He paused another moment and looked me over. "A handsome boy, a hit with the ladies, I imagine?"

"I do what I can."

"Wife?"

I laughed disparagingly.

"Someone you love."

"No."

"Oh, you are a cold fish. You won't get far in this life without a woman. This we can take care of for you." He smiled at me facetiously. "Too handsome to be a fighter, though."

"Don't judge a book by its cover."

He smiled again.

"Good advice." He tightened his grip and pulled me closer to him. He was strong, stronger than I would have guessed. He stopped walking and so I stopped. He made eye contact with me.

"You've got a question? Well go on, I can see it on your face. Ask it."

"Why do they call the ship 'Dark Agnes'?"

"What? What kind of question is this?"

"The name of the boat?"

He laughed.

"How the hell should I know? What a question. Probably the previous owner's dirty little secret, if you get my meaning."

I did, but I didn't say anything; I was preoccupied by the fact that Maneki had come out of some dark crevice and was now sitting, licking his paw, on the steel catwalk in front of us. He looked at me, then stood up and walked away into the shadows.

"Kendall? Hello in there!" Pink tapped me on the head with his fingertip.

"Don't ever touch me like that again."

Pink just stared at me, bewildered.

"Just seemed like you left the ship for a moment."

"I was thinking about when you might get to the point about why I'm here."

He scratched his chin and looked me over. His blue eyes flared with a confidence that would be unsettling for most.

"You're here to fight and fight you will, my friend. Follow me."

He didn't say another word and led me through the bowels of the vast cruise ship. The boat was probably once an inspiration of grandeur and awe many decades ago, but now was dwarfed by its colossal successors.

As we continued to work our way along, there was a loud groan and then the great leviathan came to life as though it had been slumbering for a thousand years. With a powerful jerk which almost shook me from my feet, Dark Agnes started to move.

"We're moving. Where are we going?"

"Out to open waters."

"Why."

"Privacy, of course. Arnie is always discrete. Come. I'll show you the rest."

He led me into a room that had been converted in order to house a large number of bleacher-style seating, with a handful of private VIP boxes looking down on the boxing ring. If you could even call it that at all, as the 'ring' was really nothing more than a sunken pit about four feet lower than the rest of the cold steel floor.

"You'll box bare-knuckle, not even tape is allowed. You'll be shirtless as well and you'll wear standard trunks. Proper boxing shoes will be provided." He walked around the perimeter of the ring. The overhead lighting illuminated the scattered spots of blood from previous fights.

"There is a referee, but he doesn't do much except count to ten. He doesn't have to do much; if you throw a kick, a knee, a head butt or anything else of the like, you'll never fight again. The others will make sure of that. If you win you'll fight again and as many as three times in a night. If you lose, well, you get the picture. It's brutal but there's money to be had and it's good. Come on, I'll show you your bunk."

I left the room behind Pink and played "follow the leader" once again. The room I was to stay in for the night housed 20 other bunks and a set of lockers. There was a makeshift gym set up with a few various bags, weights, mats, and jump ropes. There were other fighters. Some of them were resting and others were working out with the equipment.

"These quarters are for new fighters. You do well and we'll set you up with something better. You'll have about an hour or so before things get started. Rest, exercise, whatever suits you. Just make sure you're ready when the time comes."

Pink took a look around the room at the fighters and then walked out. I climbed up onto an empty bunk. There was no reason at this point to practice. An hour wouldn't change anything. I was in this thing all the way, with whatever skills I already had.

Rusty was shadowboxing. His Form suddenly appeared to me as a black raccoon. Stentinowski was sitting up in his bunk. He looked nervous. His Form was a grey coyote. He was rubbing the palms of his hands back and forth over his thighs, trying to warm them up. It was too early for that kind of nonsense. I laid back. I shut my eyes and went someplace else.

CHAPTER 8

Pugilism

If a punch is delivered properly, knuckles tear through flesh as though it were wet newspaper. My first throw was like that. I caught the Turk square below the cheekbone after a short dance of pleasantries. I wasn't the first in and wouldn't be the last.

I volunteered to fight. My hand went up in the air like I knew the answer to a math question. That's how it worked though; someone beat someone else, and then another fighter filled the void.

The Turk looked meaner than he actually was and his timing was off. When I got close to him, I could smell a faint scent of whisky on his breath, which can provide just enough of an edge in a game like this.

Our eyes weren't the same colour but they glowed with the same hate. Our focused steps taken in each other's direction blotted out the other bodies in the crowd, as if we

47

were the only two people in the room. When I threw the right cross, I knew even before it connected that the sap never had a chance. He hit the ground and the impact momentarily silenced the room. For me though, it was as if someone had turned the volume dial up and all I could hear was victory.

My second match came 20 minutes later and lasted only three rounds. I fought a burley Southerner who counted on landing haymakers but only ended up counting sheep on the naked steel floor. A haymaker is a fool's errand, a long shot, a Hail Mary. A good pugilist knows this. The best of them wait with a snake's patience and take small bites out of their opponents, filling them with the venom of fatigue.

I fought two more fights that night and won mostly unscathed. Rusty won his first two fights as well. He had a quiet viciousness that came unexpectedly. The selection of fighters was weak, or at least for me it was, and it seemed it was for Rusty as well.

After my last victory, Arnie waved me upstairs. I stepped through the door and into his VIP suite. Pink was there along with a group of men in suits and a few of Arnie's girls. Pink was holding a crystal glass that was half-full of whisky. He carved his lips up at me and formed an insincere smile.

"You did good work tonight son."

I nodded my thanks to Pink.

"I had a lot of money on you Kendall and you did not disappoint," he added, taking a drink from his glass. He slouched back into the soft leather of the couch. He had girls on either side of him who were draped over his body, one of which had slid her hand inside his shirt and was running it down his chest.

"I love when a fighter volunteers. It is always the best tactic for new blood to show they have no fear. Right, girls?"

The two girls rubbed their bodies over his and nodded in unison.

I was still a little out of breath and was soaked with sweat and blood. Arnie handed me a glass.

"Sit, have a drink with us. Let me introduce you to a female."

I took a seat and Arnie poured a generous portion of whisky into my glass. A young dark-haired girl slid onto my lap and started dragging her fingers along my sweating skin.

"You like, baby?" She fumbled with the English words.

Arnie grabbed her by the arm with just enough firmness to intimidate her.

"Don't talk, just sit. Let him watch the last fight."

The girl did as she was told. I took a sip of whisky. It felt nice on my dry tongue. I pushed the girl to one side and leaned forward in my chair. She slinked up onto the arm of the chair and pouted a little at my disinterest in her. It was her job to entertain me and if she failed, she had Arnie to answer to.

The bell for the final fight of the night was about to ring. The fighters were Rusty and Stentinowski. Stentinowski stretched his arms behind his back and looked good and ready for the match. Rusty was smiling at him and looked loose and confident. In fact, he looked too confident.

The bell rang and Stentinowski approached cautiously, while Rusty moved in quickly, almost flagrantly. Stentinowksi easily landed a solid right hook and Rusty staggered backwards, shaking his head.

Rusty continued to flout his defensive tactics and Stentinowski did not waste any opportunity. He landed continuous jabs and then almost connected with an uppercut, which Rusty narrowly avoided.

Stentinowski continued to land jabs and Rusty continued to let him. Rusty never faltered though. Stentinowski grew more and more confident and his footwork became sloppy. He started to get in too close, thinking he had Rusty under his thumb. I realized Stentinowski had not managed to land anything with weight other than the original right hook.

I watched as Rusty seemed to barely avoid Stentinowski's advances. He even allowed the odd punch to graze him slightly. Rusty was drawing him in, allowing his inflated confidence to grow and it was working. Stentinowski attempted a jab and Rusty feigned contact, acting dazed. Stentinowski moved in to finish him, throwing a powerful roundhouse. Rusty suddenly came alive and avoided the punch. He corked Stentinowski with a fierce straight and then a left hook. Stentinowski's nose started to flow with blood.

Rusty advanced on him and hammered him with a barrage of punches and combinations, all of which hit their mark. As Stentinowski went down, the referee started to count him out. The fight was done, or at least I thought it was; somehow Stentinowski pulled himself back up onto his feet. He staggered towards Rusty, who was smiling lasciviously.

Rusty rushed forward and put a horrific punch into Stentinowski's throat, then pummeled him in the face. Rusty sent another bone crushing roundhouse into Stentinowski's left ear. Stentinowski remained on his feet. I watched the crowd as they screamed and howled. Rusty had worked the audience into a frenzied state. He jabbed at Stentinowski, toying with him and the crowd until their frenzy morphed into a vicious blood lust.

It was at this point, I noticed Maneki sitting amongst the crowd of people. He was watching the fighters and then looked up at me. I made no gesture of acknowledgement, nor did the cat. I turned my attention back to the fight. Rusty and Stentinowski shifted into their Forms and I watched as a black raccoon approached a grey coyote. Then they were human once more.

Stentinowksi still had enough left in him to throw a few wild punches that were slow and could have been telegraphed by a child. Rusty danced around him, poking at him, prodding him. Then he stopped and hit Stentinowski with an uppercut that shattered his jaw and followed it with another roundhouse into his right temple. Stentinowski's feet gave way beneath him, and his legs seemed to almost crumble like Greek columns. He fell limply to his knees and then toppled over to his back. The fight was now over. The audience roared their approval. I looked over the room and watched as a sea of various Forms flashed sporadically.

Rusty went over to Stentinowski and crouched down beside him. He opened Stentinowski's mouth and reached inside and yanked out one of his canine teeth that he had loosened during the fight. He hoisted his hand in the air, pinching the tooth between his thumb and forefinger. Stentinowski's blood ran down his palm. The audience began to chant his name. Arnie sidled up beside me and took a drink from his glass.

"He's something, isn't he?"

"Yup."

"He doesn't have your talent, but what he lacks in skill he more than makes up for in ferocity and cleverness."

I nodded. I watched as they lifted Stentinowski's body off the floor. Two men carted him out the room and as they did, his head turned limply to the side. His eyes opened and they looked right at me, but they were devoid of any life. I scoured the room for Shrikun. There were none. I had witnessed the death of my first grey.

Arnie put his hand on my shoulder.

"Come with me."

He introduced me to a bunch of other crooks who thought their designer suits could magically transform them into legitimate businessmen, kind of the same way crooked cops think a uniform suddenly transforms them into veracious citizens. Truth is, there are no honest successful businessmen, not really. You don't get rich by doing things by the book, whether you're on the street or work for a legitimate organization. The only difference is that when you work for a genuine company, you get to look honest after you have the money, by holding charity events and fundraisers for cancer.

Arnie was smooth though. He could talk flight patterns around his contemporaries until they thought they were landing first-class in sunny Bora Bora, when in fact, Arnie had sold them an economy flight to shitty St. Louis.

He made it sound like he'd known me my whole life, and that he had been saving my debut for just the right occasion. He was happy and you could tell that by the way he drank his booze, which was carelessly. People only drink carelessly if they're really happy or really sad. Arnie was the former, somewhat because I won all my fights and beat my opponents easily, but mostly because out of the three men who were listed as his fighters tonight, he and Pink had only put markers down on me. I had made them a substantial amount of money.

Arnie took me aside for a moment.

"Go with Pink, he'll get you paid. Be here tomorrow. I have other work for you if you want it."

I nodded. Pink was already outside the room, waiting for me on the catwalk.

"Come with me, son."

We started walking along the catwalk. Beneath us, a group of men walked in the opposite direction and spoke Russian, or at least I think it was Russian. I couldn't really hear them. Pink put his arm around me.

"No one stays up late anymore. You ever notice that?"

"Nope."

He stopped walking and because he had his arm around my shoulders I was forced to stop as well. He looked me in the eye.

"The streets are empty these days. No one goes out anymore. You saying you haven't noticed?"

"Don't really care."

"Boy, you really are a fighter."

He started walking again and I stopped him.

"Are you saying I lack sophistication?" I looked hard and mean at him. He smiled up at me, unmoved by my temperament.

"Relax, no reason to get prickly with me. Just saying people don't make merry like they used to. Makes me a little nostalgic for the old days."

"I'm too young for the 'old days'."

He laughed.

"I remember this party in '74, never forget it. What a time I had and not a body under the roof was using. Sure we were drinking but we were all having such a time, we didn't even need the help. People used to know how to party."

He took his arm from around my shoulder so he could better animate his point. We kept walking.

"Music was great and everyone had long hair, men too." He slowed a little and looked up at me with conviction in his eyes. "And women knew how to fuck. They didn't have all these radical notions floating around in their skulls confusing them. It made it so much easier to liberate them from their druthers." He snickered. "I love this word, druthers, sounds so amusing to me."

"That so?"

"Yeah, that's so." There was irritation in his tone.

"The only good thing I know that came out of the seventies was Star Wars."

He groaned. "You're a pain in the ass. Do you hear me?"

"Unfortunately you're all I hear."

He shook his head and stopped walking.

"In here."

We stepped into a small room. There were four men with high-powered MK 17 SCAR assault rifles. How this weapon even made it into the country was beyond me. The men carrying the weapons appeared to be mercenaries or ex-military of some kind; they exuded that certain confidence mixed with absolute unquestioning subjugation.

Pink ignored them completely and they in turn did the same to him. In fact, Pink seemed to be oblivious to their very existence and wore a lighthearted smile on his lips as he busied himself.

"Here we are."

Pink punched in a code onto a keypad on the wall, and the entire wall gave way to reveal a hidden walk-in room. He entered it and went to a large safe that would rival any state-of-the-art bank safe. He entered a combination and then put his eye up to a monitor. A flash of light made a retinal scan of his eye, like something right out of movie. The safe made a not-so-subtle shifting sound and Pink pulled on the large handle of the door. It opened.

Unable to contain my curiosity, I stepped forward. Inside were mountains of cash in various currencies. Pink went over to a stack of Canadian bills and grabbed a small brick of cash.

"Come in here."

I stepped inside.

"Will this keep you busy for a while?"

The stack he handed me was easily five grand, in hundred dollar bills.

"Looks good to me."

"Good. Step outside."

Pink closed the vault door and spun the activation wheel, resetting the combination and security protocols of the vault. I started to leave.

"Where you going? You bored with me?"

"A little," I chuckled "Going back to the party."

"There's a good lad."

I walked out. Pink called after me.

"Do me a favour and make that brunette's dreams come true for me, will ya?"

"Handle your own business, Pink and I'll handle mine."

"Don't be such a poor sport, Kendall."

He hollered something else at me, but I was too far out of earshot and the reverberation on the ship's hull made it impossible to make out his words. I had an idea though.

CHAPTER 9

Bump in the Night

It was one thing to have won the fight, but the real battle began at the party afterwards. A thousand vices were waiting for us, looking as pretty as a Friday night whore; unmarked coloured pills sat in bowls like an emptied packet of Skittles. People dipped their mitts in and swallowed their catch, titillated by the unknown effects their chosen poison would have on them.

There was an Everest of cocaine, Ecstasy, acid, meth, and more. Arnie knew what people wanted. They wanted sport, to go hunting. They wanted blood and Arnie gave it to them every second Friday night, for a small price. After their lust for blood was sated, he gave them a jungle filled with preying eyes and minds that were cooking on whatever substance that was made available to them. Arnie always had a fresh crop of young girls readily available, not a single one of whom could speak a word of English, yet they could giggle and fidget as they tried.

I never fell victim to a single one of the vices Arnie tried to clamp shut around me that first night. I came close a couple of times, but managed to find my way into the open night air after we had docked. I thought I had gone unnoticed too, but I was wrong. Arnie had noticed and told me so later. I thought about that, about him watching me. I realized if I wanted this new thing to work, like any other job, I needed to be a team player no matter what that meant.

I picked up a bottle of whiskey. I thought that's what a person does when they ought to celebrate. I had money in my pocket, so why not. I walked out into the night with my paper-bagged prize in hand and took a deep swig. It felt good going down. It's odd how alcohol going into your belly makes your wounds feel better but burns mercilessly when it runs freely over the wound itself.

I walked aimlessly and rather enjoyed doing so. I never paid much attention to the hands of the clock. Time would have to look for someone else to torture.

The night was quiet. I liked it quiet. I liked being able to hear the trees creak and the leaves play their tricks. I let the night air fill my lungs. I took another drink from the bottle in my hand and wiped my chin. I walked down the sidewalk for at least another hour, heading nowhere in particular. I didn't see a soul, other than a grey dog tearing at a bag of trash down an alley. I stopped and watched him wrestle with it for a few minutes. He finally noticed me and looked at me like I was invading his privacy. Then the dog became human, the dog simply being his Form, and continued to look at me speculatively. No one likes to be watched while they're eating. I moved on and let the man have his meal.

My bottle was three quarters empty when I heard them. I rounded the corner and approached the backside of a four-story tenement. The building was dilapidated, a housing project meant to breed and house predators.

It was dark as there were no streetlights on the backside of the building. I stood in the shadows and edged my nose around the corner. There were four of them standing and one poor soul lying on the dirt in front of them. Local wolves had found a piece of tender meat. I don't much care for people who hunt in packs. I find it cowardly. I set my bottle on the ground and I moved forward slowly. Their backs were to me. As I approached, one of them started beating on their victim. I didn't hear a sound. When I get like this, I don't hear anything; I stop listening with my ears and my other senses become heightened.

I put the toe of my boot into the backside of the knee of the chap I figured could handle himself the best. He bent backwards in an awkward way so his face was looking up at mine as he continued to fall. I enjoyed his look of shock. I put my elbow in his Adam's apple to quicken his trip to the ground and he was done. One of the other men looked at me with frozen eyes. Hesitation will get you killed in these situations. I put my right fist into his nose with a force that crushed it. He folded like laundry and landed just as neat in a pile in front of me.

I didn't get around quickly enough thanks to the drink in me, and I took a pipe or something like it across my back. I managed to roll with it, the whisky working to numb the pain. I put myself back on my feet in time to see the second swing come for my head. I ducked beneath the pipe as it passed over me and I came up with a left uppercut that lifted him off his feet. He landed on his back and kicked up a cloud of dust.

The fourth just looked at me and I looked at him. His eyes said he was going to run and he did, but not before he changed into his Form. A black raccoon scuttled off into the night. Normally I would have chased him to finish my work but I was drunk. Hell, it was my fifth fight of the night after all.

I straightened myself out, ran my hands through my hair, and started to walk back towards my bottle.

"Thank you."

It was a woman's voice. I turned around and squinted into the darkness. A thin figure moved towards me.

"My car broke down two streets over and my cell phone battery was dead. I left the car to look for a payphone to call a tow truck and…" She trailed off and went silent.

I couldn't quite make out her face, only rough shapes in the darkness. Now I was the one who hesitated.

"What's your name?" She had a good voice, soft and lacelike.

I fenced the question with one of my own.

"What's the make of your car?"

"Audi."

"Year?"

"Brand new, this year."

"Why don't you show me where it is?"

"Okay." Her voice was meek.

"Don't worry lady, I'm not going to rob you." I started to walk without her and then heard her pick up her feet behind me.

As we stepped into the light beneath the street lamp on the sidewalk, I got my first glimpse of her. She had a bruise starting to form on her face and there was a small bit of drying blood in the right corner of her full lips. Long dark, lashes protected her blue eyes, that glowed evenly in the soft light. I looked at her too long and I knew it but didn't care.

I let her lead. Her car wasn't far, just like she said. I told her to sit in the driver's seat and I got her to release the hood latch. I could tell the problem right away. One of the battery cables wasn't connected properly.

"Do you have any tools, or a spare tire kit in the trunk?"

She got out of the car.

"Will this help?" She handed me a folding multipurpose tool.

I unfolded it and used the pliers to tighten the loose connection.

"Okay, give it try."

She did and the engine fired. I closed the hood and saw her sitting inside the vehicle. The moment passed. I had done my job and turned and walked away.

I heard her car door open.

"What's your name?"

I turned to face her.

"Doesn't matter, does it?"

"It does to me."

I scoffed, then turned and started to walk away, but something made me stop again. This was the first good thing I'd done in a real long while. It felt weird. I turned to face her again.

"William, my name's William."

I regretted it the moment the words came out of my mouth. Real smart Willie boy, why didn't I just give her a fingerprint too? I started walking again before she could say anything else. She couldn't know me; beautiful things should stay out of my reach so they can remain that way. Walking away was another good thing I'd done that night. I thought about all the birds out there I could have had any time I wanted. I wasn't bad to look at, in fact probably better than most lowlifes around. I had a full head of sandy brown hair that was cropped short but not too short. I was lean and in good shape, I had to be. I had a man's jaw that was square with a pair of blue eyes you could be proud of, if that was your thing.

I told myself to stop thinking about her and convinced myself I had the will to do so. This was the only time in my life where I knowingly lied to myself, because I didn't stop thinking about her. Not that night or any night after it.

I made my way back to the spot where I had left my bottle on the ground but when I got there, the only thing left was the brown paper bag.

CHAPTER 10

Pleasantries and Things
Not so Pleasant at All

I sat, perched upon my stool, and swiveled back to the rail of the bar. The bartender went by the name of Mex. He was a good man, considering he worked a bar on a boat for a man named Arnie with a crowd of crooks. He wasn't a talker, but that was because he was missing his tongue. It had been cut out of his mouth years ago. He was a damn good listener though, and it was a safe bet he'd never say anything unkind about you to your face or behind your back.

Mex handed me a glass and two ounces of decent quality bourbon to go with it. I took a whiff and then a sip, setting the glass on the counter in front of me.

Arnie was having a conversation with Rusty. Rusty might not have been aware of that though, because he just argued everything that came through Arnie's lips. Pink and I were just sitting at the bar, listening and drinking.

"You don't like the way I fight?'

Arnie shook his head calmly. "You misunderstand me."

"Do I?"

Arnie had very limited patience for direct disobedience. His was a unique society, with certain rules and doctrines, and he required that no one question these orders. In fact, after you were spoon-fed his lies with coercive manipulation, he would nonchalantly ask you to forget what you had just talked about in the first place. It was beautiful in its simplicity. Get someone to believe what you want him or her to believe then make that person think you were just making idle conversation.

Once you've learned something, it is almost impossible to unlearn it. Even in school, they teach you that there are only five human senses: touch, taste, smell, sight, and sound. Whatever happened to that other one we call common sense? Why is this the sense that every government, military, and form of media want you to forget exists? Maybe it's because it's the only sense that requires actual thought to use it, and therefore a dangerous thing; a single individual can undo the work of a thousand drones.

Arnie was getting irritated. "Yes, you heard me." I could see his temper flare.

"I won the fight, didn't I? Got this sweet chain made last night to celebrate." Rusty was referring to a necklace he wore that had Stentinowksi's tooth hanging from it. He had someone make a two-inch silver shaft with the tooth hilted on the end. He had the tooth lightly beveled so he could use it to snort cocaine with.

"I wanted seven rounds and you gave me five."

"I gave you a victory, that's what you said you wanted! Go fuck yourself!"

Arnie ran his hand through his thin dark hair once slowly, then two more times quickly. Pink and I swiveled in our chairs to face the action that was about to take place.

Arnie went over to the end of the bar. He tapped his index finger twice on the edge of the counter and Mex handed him a 9 mm and a full clip. Arnie put the clip in and pulled a bullet into the chamber. He walked over to Rusty.

"This is not a democracy. You do as I say or your useless brain gets renovated. Do you follow?"

Rusty stood up with the nozzle of the pistol pressed firmly against his forehead and looked Arnie directly in the eyes.

"Well, what are you waiting for?"

This was an unexpected move from Rusty. As it turns out, he wasn't dumb as much as he was mentally ill. It's truly strange when you think about it: a man beats another man to a bloody pulp, enjoys killing him, and extracts a tooth from his mouth as a souvenir and we don't think to ourselves, hey, this guy might just be unbalanced. But in the world we were living in, this was the new normal.

Arnie pulled the gun from his head. He knew Rusty had him, but only for a moment. Crazy people had necessities too and Arnie only needed a split second to find Rusty's weakness.

"Pink, take this piece of shit and get him off my boat."

Pink shot back the rest of his drink and stood up off the stool. Rusty looked at Arnie. Then he realized what was happening. Arnie wasn't going to kill him, no, that wouldn't work. He was going to take away the thing he loved the most, the fights.

"So I can't fight for you anymore?"

"I can always find good fighters. Dime a dozen."

Rusty rubbed his head and then sighed.

"Okay, fine. You're the boss. You want seven rounds, I'll give you seven rounds."

Arnie turned back to face Rusty.

"You don't want to know what will happen to you if you question me again. Understood?"

"Yeah, fine. Can we eat now?"

Arnie looked over at Pink, who shrugged at Rusty's seemingly random suggestion.

"I could eat." Pink looked over at me. "You hungry?"

"Whatever."

Sometimes, ambivalence is the only emotion worth having.

CHAPTER 11

2003 – Harvest

They brought her in with the other nine girls who could not be mistaken for women. A trivial semantic that Arnie would remedy shortly. It's amazing how trashy make-up, a short skirt, and heels can add ten years to the illusion of maturity. Each girl was a different ethnicity, like they had been handpicked from a human supermarket.

I made eye contact with one of them. She was young but she had hardened eyes of coal, the kind you'd imagine a wolf would have facing down the barrel of a shotgun in the hands of Allan Quartermain. She bared her canines and snarled with a ferocity that shook the other girls from their zombie-like state. She had claws too, and she raked at her captors with them. She writhed and squirmed for no other reason than it was her nature to do so. Arnie hit her with a

OF VIOLENCE AND CLICHÉ

closed fist and she dropped to her knees. A lethargic stream of gooey blood trickled from her mouth.

I watched. I sat at the bar and nursed a glass of bourbon. I had won all three fights that night. Despite the victories, they were difficult and vicious rounds. Either I was slowing down or my opponents were getting much better. I was in no shape to stand and my stomach was not ready for any of Arnie's tender love and care.

Arnie stood her up and held her loosely by her throat. Their eyes locked and she spit right in his face. I liked her. Arnie liked her too so he hit her again, this time in the gut. She doubled over and coughed blood onto the floor beneath her. I spoke up.

"Would you cut off the hands of your prize fighter right before he's about to make you thousands of dollars?"

Arnie ran both of his hands along the sides of his head to straighten his damp, disheveled hair. He took a small vial from his pocket and dipped his elongated pinky nail into the white powder, which he vacuumed into his left nostril. He coughed and laughed at the same time.

"Kendall is right, never harm that which will bring you profit. I should know better. Still…" He paused and took another sniff of powder before he continued. He locked his eyes with mine and I watched the fire behind them smolder and erupt into pure coca driven lust. "Young meat is so much better once it has been tenderized."

He cracked his knuckles and smiled at me.

"Get them cleaned up and get some chow in them. I want them schooled and ready in a week. Break their spirits but not their bones, Rusty."

Eight of the girls kept their eyes to the floor. If you kick a dog long enough, he won't bare his teeth. Hell, after a long while he'll probably love you for it. These girls were young, and their young minds were telling them to settle in for the ride, follow the rules and survive. But the girl with the hardened eyes and claws looked straight ahead, past the pain, anger and fear, past Arnie and right at me. Her eyes burned a hole through the glass of bourbon I held in front of my mouth. Her eyes spoke volumes, but mine gave her back nothing. I had gotten good at that, hiding my tells. I was a master at it, actually. I had to be. I just looked back at her with veiled emotion, but I still felt something deep down.

Rusty was the wrong man for this job. I knew it, and I just needed Arnie to realize it too. I saw an open window and decided to try and climb inside.

Rusty led the queue from the room and I went back to my bourbon. Arnie sat down on the stool beside me and Mex brought him a shot of Stoli. He put it back and fingered for another.

"Women will always be at our feet."

I knew better than to engage him when he got like this.

"Because we have a willingness to do the things they won't," he continued.

I took another drink and set my empty glass on the counter. I knew he hadn't finished yet. I could feel his eyes on me. I waited a moment and then I looked at him like he wanted me too. His eyes searched mine.

"Why'd you say what you did when I hit her?"

"What do you mean?" I knew to answer a question like that with another question.

"I mean, why should you give a shit if I tap a bitch back into line?"

"I want to get paid," I said, looking right back into his eyes steadily.

He looked down at his full shot glass. He took it between his thumb and forefinger, brought it to his mouth and his lips parted slightly. They disgusted me; I couldn't help but imagine all the filthy places they'd been, let alone the deplorable things they'd said.

"You want to get paid. You mean the fights aren't enough? Is that it?"

"I mean I want more."

He smiled.

"Of course you do. Don't we all." He put back the shot and wiped his mouth.

"Okay." He got up from the stool. "I'll take care of it. You want to work, so you'll work. I like ambition."

As he walked away, I pushed my empty glass along the counter and Mex responded with another long pour.

"Oh, Kendall?"

I turned in my stool to face Arnie.

"You'll still do the fights, got it?"

I nodded as he faded through the door. I swiveled back to the bar and Mex had left the full bottle in front of me.

CHAPTER 12

Arrivals

On Sundays, I would take a cab out of the city. It was my time away and the closest thing I'd ever have to a trip of my own, even though it was just for a few hours. No one knew about these departures, not even Arnie. It took about 45 minutes to get to Pearson from the downtown core. I'd direct the driver towards Terminal 1, International Arrivals and head into the airport. I would sit and watch, usually alone, as anyone who's got a heart would be standing and waiting for their loved ones to arrive. That's what I was there for: the arrivals.

Husbands came home to warm embraces and filled their arms up with jubilant children. Military men made it back and said nothing at all, wrestling within themselves to find a way to touch again while walking away silently, holding hands with their lover. Teenagers came back from their first taste of the world, sun-kissed skin glowing, brown locks bleached light and with optimism about the future in their eyes, and relief in their parent's.

The holidays were particularly special. There were amiable handshakes and hugs fired like Colts in all directions. Family traveled from all over the world from distant countries or neighbouring provinces, it didn't really matter because they all came to break bread and be together.

Maybe I sugar-coated it all a little for my own benefit, maybe it wasn't all a perfect celluloid reflection, but it was damn near close. Mine was a life of struggle, but out there watching everyone else I could feel something that could be misconstrued as hope. This could keep my own heart beating beneath my ribs and my head in the game. A man can lose himself altogether and one day, well, he just isn't there anymore.

Life skips certain people on a few things. I know what I had to do to survive. I wouldn't ever have what these people had. I'd made choices and couldn't go back in time to undo them. I knew what I was. I knew what I was doing. Still, it didn't mean I cared not for a little goodness now and again. If that made me soft, I could live with that.

"You're early."

"No, you're late."

The man's name was Dietrich. He sat down beside me and pulled the tab back on his coffee cup lid. He took a discerning sip and his lips puckered from the heat. Minutes passed and he said nothing. He just watched the people come and go, beside me.

I started meeting Dietrich years ago, in the airport bar. He would order a scotch and soda and I a whisky. We drank and talked. This had become a habit and soon we agreed upon a day or two each month to get together. He kept his blond hair neat, almost militant. He had a long face and was always clean-shaven. It was a good face by all accounts. On this day, he wore a grey suit similar to the ones cops wear when they don't want to look like cops.

Dietrich set his coffee on the marble floor and looked back at the next batch of arrivals. I didn't look at him but could make out the semblance of an honest smile in my peripheral view.

"You been here long?" he asked, reaching down for his cooling coffee.

"I lost track of time, so I couldn't say."

"I see." He paused to take a sip of coffee. "How's your record?"

I smiled. Dietrich knew I was a boxer of some kind. Normally I wouldn't tell someone my business, any of it, but it's hard to keep making up stories about cut lips and black eyes.

"Been a rough week actually, but I came out on top."

"Seems you always do."

"So far, but there's no place but down from the top, isn't that what they say?"

He smiled in response, but kept watching the crowd of people collecting their luggage and loved ones. He took another sip and finally seemed pleased with the temperature.

There was a brief moment of silence and then he spoke up again.

"I have something for you." Dietrich reached into his inside coat pocket and took a rectangular object, wrapped in plain yellow paper. He set it down on the wide armrest of the chair.

"Open it."

I unwrapped the package and inside was a small chess-board.

"Have you ever played before?"

I said I hadn't.

"It is not unlike your boxing. It takes patience, strategy, a calculating mind and ends in violence." He said the last part with a laugh.

Dietrich explained the rules and we played a few games, all of which I mostly stumbled through and lost terribly. We talked some more about nothing at all and watched our arrivals. Hours passed and so did new matches of chess. Dietrich was right, it was like boxing and I fell in love with it instantly. For once, win or lose, things didn't end up with me bleeding all over myself.

CHAPTER 13

Interrogation

Pattys can fight. That's one stereotype that I've witnessed to be true. Bastards toss even better when they're drunk. It's something of a paradox really. Put them in front of a tussle and they won't quit until the job is done, but give them a job and they won't lift a finger.

I didn't catch the fighter's name, but his first punch got through my defense and I felt my solar plexus go soft. He'd been leading with lefts for some time and then hammered me with a dynamite right cross to the kisser. I sacrificed my defensive position to land a firm cross of my own on his jawbone. I felt it break, but still he was able to plant a concrete fist into the soft flesh that was once my solar plexus, and I felt something rupture. He saw me wince and moved in for the kill flagrantly, his eyes filled with brazen ferocity. Overconfidence was his undoing, and I put all my force into a haymaker, which I know I said was a fool's errand, but sometimes with the right planning and a little luck, it works. I sent the six-and-a-half foot Irishman staggering until his own feet tangled in a ridiculous fashion and he went down.

I didn't watch the ref count. I didn't need to. I couldn't hear a thing, but I could see the salivating crowd, and smell my victory all over my body and in the air around me.

I saw Arnie and Pink watching me and I raised my arms skyward. At that very moment, the volume rushed back into my ears and everything came alive again for me. The crowd wanted more, so much more. I knew another fight would kill me, and Arnie knew this too. Arnie was a lot of things, but he was no fool and he knew fighting. He watched each footstep with microscopic dissection. He left all emotion out of it and watched the look each man wore on his face and the intensity in their eyes. He was able to decide the outcome of every match with remarkable accuracy before the first punch had even been thrown.

He called the night despite the outstanding match, stating aloud that it wasn't possible that another fight could match the strength of its predecessor and why belittle that. It helped that he offered everyone a free round. The room was promptly flooded with cleavage and silver trays of splash.

I knew the expectation was that I'd leave the floor unaided to maintain the pretence of the triumphant gladiator. Once behind the curtain, I collapsed from internal bleeding, among other things. There were muffled sounds and distorted lights. Legs danced all around me and then there was nothing.

When I woke I was on a hospital bed but I was not in a hospital. I was covered with blankets up to my neck, keeping me warm. There was a saline drip and needle in my arm. I lay there in the centre of the dressing room where the night had begun.

Arnie always had two doctors on call. They were good doctors, not like the down-and-outers you see in films that depict situations similar to mine. They simply had their own vices, which at some point Arnie had exploited. They now owed him.

There was a box with a signal button by my left hand, which I pushed. Moments later, the doctor came into the dressing room, asked me a few standard questions and put a light in each eye.

"How long until I'm back on the floor, doc?"

"Let's start with back on your feet, okay?"

"Okay, so when will I be back on my feet?"

"Two or three days, as long as you rest now."

I felt my body ease into exhaustion. The doctor inserted a needle into the tube that was feeding my arm, adding another drug to my saline drip. I started to slide off into the void where everything was white; the world had bled me out.

Hours later, the light flooded into my pupils. It felt like I'd been asleep for years. My head throbbed as I tried to re-gain my focus. The girl that Arnie had brought in the other night was sitting on the bench in front of me. She looked like a mirage through my glassy eyes. She had one black eye, evidence of Arnie's violence against her. I smiled a sick smile, as I knew he wouldn't let that stop her from working.

We looked at each other. I could tell she was sizing me up, reading my face. I knew I couldn't let her have anything. I couldn't give anything away.

"You think you can hide yourself from me, is that it?"

Her eyes pierced mine like pushpins and her words caught me off guard. No one had ever done that, not even Arnie.

"You're starting to recover." Her accent was thick.

"Your English is good," I said, changing the subject.

"Don't do that." She pulled her knees up into her chest as though she suddenly felt a chill.

"Look, I'm tired. Give me the day and come back on Sunday, okay?"

"It is Sunday."

"It is?"

"Yes."

It was like that. Days just disappeared like they had never existed in the first place.

"So what are you doing here? What do you want from me?" I asked.

"Just to talk."

"To talk. About what?"

"Whatever."

"I don't do that."

"Everyone does that."

"Not me. Listen kid, you should take off. You shouldn't be in here."

She let her tiny feet fall back to the floor. They were bare and innocent, like those of a young child.

"You can leave. I mean, if you wanted to, you could just walk out of here and never come back. But me, I am an ocean away from my home, in a place God does not know about." She looked away from me for only a moment, and then seemed to pull herself together. "I have no passport, no friends or family, no money. Even if I could leave, it would be useless. They would find me and kill me. But you have money. You are a citizen. Why do you stay?" She looked at me, searchingly.

"I'm a fighter, kid. I don't know anything else, so I fight."

"Arnie pays you?"

"He does."

"Do you kill?"

"That's never my intention."

Her eyes traveled towards the ceiling as she gave some thought to what I'd just said.

"I'm afraid. I know what's to come and I am really afraid."

Tears welled up in her eyes, which pleaded with mine. This time I was stronger and gave her nothing. She was too, and forced the tears back deep inside.

"I can't help you even if I wanted to," I said, flatly.

"I know." She smiled a fake smile.

"Look kid, some of the girls take something to help them through the first time. Others take something all the time." I knew right away that she wouldn't take a damn thing. She'd fight and wrestle her way through it. She wouldn't last long; the bold ones never do.

"Can I come talk to you again?"

"No."

"Maybe tomorrow?"

"Don't."

She smiled a real smile this time and it was honest. I knew that I was seeing the last of a girl that soon would be gone forever. No one, not even her closest family would ever recognize her again, not that they would even get the chance. She got up from the bench and started to leave the room.

"What's your name, kid?"

"Danika. Yours?"

"Kendall."

"No it isn't." She smiled that same defiant grin again and left the room.

I had lost my very first fight to a girl.

CHAPTER 14

Déjà Vu

It's been said that there are two things that can save a man's soul and two things that can just as easily condemn it; women and rock and roll can keep a man alive or bury him, but I don't really believe in that kind of romantic horseshit. For me, there are only two things that'll keep me out of the ground, and those are my right and left hands. Even then, it's not a sure thing.

You have to quickly learn the rules of the yard. If you want to beat a bully, you can't outsmart him. Unfortunately, there's no clever way to stop the beatings. Sure, if your tongue has enough silver on it, you can chirp your way out of a few scrapes, but eventually, they'll keep on coming. The only way to end getting your ass kicked is to step into him; beat him so hard, so mercilessly, and put fear into his heart. A good walloping isn't enough. He'll find you the next day and beat you harder than before, because all you managed to do was to make him angry. I call it the hornet's nest theory.

How you handle a bully translates into the way you handle moments of violence for the rest of your life. In a fight, you really only have two options. You either out-box the man or you make him fear you. No matter the force with which you hit him, the impact is twice as hard if a man has fear in his heart. I've seen many fall because an opponent outfoxed him with his eyes. While it's typically said of a woman, a man can just as readily send another man to ruin with just a glance.

Musings, that's what I have when I drink. Most people drink to forget, to live in the moment. I drink so I can be alone with my thoughts and unscramble the eggs. I had been sitting at the bar in a place uptown, the name of which I couldn't remember, drinking whiskey for hours and thinking. The barman has been good to me. You know the sort; he was generous with his pours and no bullshit "Hey, Pal" conversations.

I was to meet Fletcher Fielding. His name was right out of a book and he was Arnie's contact on the outside. My job tonight was to give him a list of women that had been earmarked for importing, who were mostly Romanian from the look of things. Although Arnie hadn't told me these details, I had looked for myself in the package of papers Arnie had given to me to carry. Knowing kept me on top of things.

I had never met Fletcher and today was the first time Arnie had mentioned his name. I felt pretty confident in Arnie's trust for me with this job. More importantly, I was sitting in an uptown bar filled with people who slept in clean linen sheets, wore overpriced cologne, adorned their napes with fancy rocks and lived taxable lives. This meant only one of two things with regards to Fletcher; either he thought there was no better place to meet than away from the typical lower class elements associated with Arnie's line of business, or more likely, Fletcher was a clean-sheet man himself. Not that I really cared; I was drinking Jack when it should have been fine bourbon but it was still on Arnie's dime.

This particular upscale joint was busy. The noise was at a buzzing level so that conversations could be heard by the people engaged in them and yet still remain private. There were a few empty seats at the bar, but it had four sides and was large enough that the barman could have benefitted from two assistants on a night like this. I figured his pace would help keep me sober enough for my meeting. I had a gentleman sitting next to me who was drinking Limey Gimlets. He looked like a Brit too. His chin kept crashing against his sternum like an Australian wave during the stormy season, so I knew his ears had shut off. I kept the seat to my right free, telling the odd adventurer that I was meeting someone.

I watched the barman pour another drink for the Yorkie, who had inadvertently managed to muster enough coordination to tap the rim of his empty glass in the barman's presence. I tried the same trick and tapped my empty glass as well, but he avoided my gesture and took an order from a group of Suits who had just set the colour of their money on the mahogany. Their colours were brighter than mine.

"You should do the same if you want Mike to notice you."

The sound of a female voice addressing me was startling. I looked to my right and a woman in a red crepe sleeveless dress slid her firm beautiful body into the empty chair beside me. I stared at her legs long and hard, partly because she was beautiful but mostly because I had seen this pair of stems before. Then I noticed she was smiling at me.

"Now I know it's you. You did the same thing two years ago," she said. Her lips were parted in a way that led me to believe she was about to smile.

"Excuse me?" I responded. At least I think I said something like that.

"You don't remember me. It was a long time ago, I guess."

She crossed her legs and I looked directly at her.

"I remember you."

"You do?" She became a little vulnerable. I remained stone-faced.

"Yeah I saw you on TV once. You're an actress, right?"

She looked disappointed and started to get up to leave. I gently put my hand on her arm to stop her.

"How's the car?"

She stared at me with a bewildered look. I don't know why I did it. Maybe it was because she looked disappointed. Maybe it was because I wanted to feel what it felt like to talk to someone like her or maybe it was because she was warm and was so damn beautiful. Maybe it was all of the reasons at once.

She sat back down and ordered a drink.

"The car is in the shop, actually. Bad gasket or something like that. It will probably cost me upwards of five hundred dollars."

"If it does, switch mechanics."

"Okay, I will." She looked down at her drink and smiled a little, playing with her glass and rotating it around in a circle. "I really thought I'd never see you again."

I didn't know what to say but found it impossible to conceal what I was feeling. She fidgeted in her chair a little. I didn't say anything and took a drink. She kept looking at me and although I didn't look back at her, I knew there was hurt and disappointment in her eyes.

"I'm sorry. I shouldn't have intruded. I just wanted to come over and say hello."

She got up and walked away. I took a drink and cursed under my breath, and told myself I was doing the right thing by letting her go. I did it once before and it was right then, but at this moment it really felt completely wrong. I left my drink, got up and went after her. I moved through the crowded room and put my hand on her back as I approached. She turned around to face me.

"I left you alone that night because I knew you were safe."

"Really?"

"No. That's not true. I left you because I had to. The circumstances were bad. I saw you, what you were wearing, the kind of car you were driving and I knew that I came from a different place than you."

"You made a poor assumption about me, then. You are making another one now. I just wanted to come say hello because you had stopped those men and helped me."

"That's a crock of shit."

"You've got no right to talk to me like that." Her eyes were indignant but mine had a fierceness that took the light out of hers.

"Look lady, you don't know a thing about me, where I come from, or the things I've done. If I walked away from you that night, I did so for reasons you could never understand."

I was angry with her and her expectations. I started to walk away and turned back around for more.

"I can't know you, I can't! And I know you didn't just come over to say hello." I lost it a little bit. Women will do this to you, but I'm thankful that I'm a man, just so I can know this feeling all the same.

She stood there in shock at what I'd just said, and then suddenly I could see her body relax.

"Have a drink with me."

"Can't. I'm meeting someone."

"I've got a table reserved. I'm meeting a friend and she's running late. Have one drink with me."

I halfheartedly followed her to her table and we sat down. She caught the server's attention and placed an order for a whisky and a glass of red wine. The skirted table was rather small and cozy.

"My name's Karen." Once she said it, I realized it didn't even matter. I felt the way I did about her and I didn't even know a thing about this woman, let alone her name.

She gestured towards my face. "Can I ask what happened?"

"No." What could I have said?

"Oh. Okay."

There was a moment's silence between us and then someone tapped me on the shoulder. It was the barman, Mike.

"There's a man at the door who says he's looking for you."

"How'd you know he was looking for me?"

"He described you." The barman allowed his irritation to show plainly.

I thanked him, and he walked away, mumbling under his breath.

"I've got to go." I got up abruptly to leave. I didn't want to be seen with her, although she didn't know that.

"Okay."

"I…" I trailed off, unsure of what else to say. I walked away, having regained my composure and focused on the task in front of me.

At the door, a man was clearly surveying the room. Fletcher was not what I had expected. He was a tall man, lanky but not uncoordinated. He had longer blonde hair with a scruffy five-day growth shadow on his face.

He also recognized me as the person he was looking for.

"Kendall, right? Let's go outside." We started out the door when Karen came around the corner.

"William! William, wait a second."

I stopped. So did Fletcher, who had a suspicious look across his face.

"I'm sorry to interrupt, but this is my address. If you're in the area again, maybe you'll stop by and say hello or something."

I took the piece of paper from her hand and tried to smile, although it probably just looked like a scowl.

Once outside, Fletcher lit a cigarette, taking a deep long drag and letting the smoke out through his nose.

"Why'd she call you William?"

"Because that's the name I gave the bird."

"Who was she? Pretty little thing." He looked back in through the window, hoping to catch another glimpse of her. I watched as his Form flickered to a black cougar for just a moment.

"Some broad who helped me pass the time while I waited for you. You're over an hour late."

"It wasn't my fault." He shifted nervously, knowing Arnie didn't like it when people were late for appointments.

"Let's start walking. I'm sick of this neighbourhood."

He did as he was told. I took the piece of paper with Karen's address written on it from my pocket, crumpled it into a ball, and tossed it into a garbage bin.

"Don't you want to know where she lives? I want to know where she lives." A sleazy grin stretched across Fletcher's face.

"I've got plenty of women who I can have whenever I want. I don't need any hassles from some uptight, uptown chick."

"I wouldn't let that one fly away."

"Shut it!" I handed him the package Arnie intended for me to give to him and left him standing at the corner. I headed underground to catch the subway, letting the city evaporate above me.

CHAPTER 15

Odds and Ends

She had been crying. She could see that I knew this and was ashamed of her tears.

"I was getting better, you know?"

I didn't say anything. I just listened. I had been walking around Dark Agnes for around half an hour. I had stopped to see Mex for a drink and then walked the catwalk some more. We had been out on the water since last night and as we made our way back to Toronto harbour with the rising sun, my stomach was starting to turn on me.

"I should have just accepted my fate by now." She looked down at her small hands and changed the subject. "I watched you fight last night."

"Did you?"

"I always watch you fight."

"That so?"

"Yes. You're good, too."

"I try."

"You know my uncle was a boxer."

"Oh yeah?"

"He used to box once month in a town not far from mine. Papa used to take me sometimes. My uncle had a lot of training. He was a very good boxer and would win most of the time."

"Sounds like my kind of guy."

"You box like him."

"I doubt it."

"What I mean is, I watch you fight and you move like him, sometimes."

"You've got a big nose, kiddo."

She touched her nose. "It's not big."

"It's a figure of speech."

"Your nose is bigger than mine in real life though."

I smiled back at her. "Sure is. Look, I gotta run. Talk to you later, okay?"

"Okay."

I walked out of the room and back onto the ship's catwalk. I was angry with myself for letting her get to me in some way. I needed to stay focused and Danika was breaking that focus with slow certainty. I tried to tell myself to stay with the fights, to keep my mind sharp and my wits about me.

I closed the door to my room. I was alone and laid down on my bed, contemplating a nap.

"She's something, isn't she?"

I jolted upright and cursed out loud.

"You can't be here! Not here, not now. Get out!"

Lamia slid her chair next to the bed and sat down, putting her feet up on the edge of the bed.

"But we were just getting comfortable."

"I'm serious. Why are you here?"

"Isn't it wonderful that you can ask me anything you like, unlike that awful tabby cat?"

I just stared at her. I did not have the patience to deal with her banter.

"Right. How many fights do you think it will take?"

"To do what?"

"Come now Willie, to get what you want, of course."

"You know something? Before I met you, I'd never seen a woman so beautiful and so naked, for that matter, that I couldn't stand looking at."

"Clever man, good for you. I can take a hint. But remember, each drop of blood will only bring you closer to an ocean of crimson. You would do well to remember that."

"I don't want your advice or your ridiculous metaphors."

"And yet I give it to you for free." She smiled facetiously.

"It's time for you to go."

"Mind if I use the door to leave?"

"Whatever, just get the hell out of here."

"See you soon, Willie."

She slipped lithely through the door and into the hallway. My hands found my face and started rubbing at my temples. She had managed to rob me of my moment alone. I decided to take out my fury on some poor unsuspecting punching bag in the gym. I needed to hit something.

CHAPTER 16

A Phone Call
Grocery List

Standing at the corner of Queen and Bathurst, I rolled a coin between my knuckles.

"Hey man, got a smoke?"

You often get asked for things on the streets of this city. I looked the interloper in the eyes.

"Nope."

"What you gonna do with that quarter?"

"Spend it, eat it, who knows?"

"Can I have it?"

"Piss off!" He buggered away a few feet before asking a young woman if she had a subway token.

I fed my coins into the slot of the payphone and heard the click of the dial tone. I punched the 10 digits that I had memorized by then. It rang three times. I had decided

I would wait for the fifth ring before hanging up. On the fourth ring, someone picked up on the other end,

"Hello?" It was her voice.

"Hello this is Kend, um, William."

"Who?"

"William. We talked a few weeks back at a bar. I can't remember the name of the place."

"I'm sorry, I don't remember. I talk to so many guys."

"You do?"

"I'm kidding. Of course I remember you. Wasn't it more like a month ago when I saw you?"

"Yes."

"What makes you think I'm available anymore?"

"What makes you think that's why I'm calling?"

"Isn't that why you're calling?"

The noise around me had intensified and a line-up had started in front of me.

"Hey buddy, you almost done with the phone?"

I cupped my hand over the mouthpiece.

"Not yet, beat it."

We made plans for Saturday night and I hung up. I started walking east on Queen Street, towards Osgoode subway station and got off at Davisville. I was in midtown and that was on purpose. Arnie had sent me on a job to pick some things up for the girls at the pharmacy in this area for various reasons, one of which was that it was far enough away from his downtown warehouse that he didn't have to worry about me being seen by someone he knew. The other reasons I'll get to in a moment.

I had gone down the wrong aisle. I just stood there staring at the myriad boxes, containers, and other assorted cosmetic products on the shelf. I was being foolish, sentimental in the strangest setting; hair dyes and hand creams, eye shadow and face powder, the most beautiful packaging filled with waxy promises. The lipsticks were lined up perfectly in dotted rows, ordered by shade and saturation. I reached out and picked up a certain brand. "Cabaret Claret" was the color code it had been given. I rolled the silver bullet around in my hand and removed the lid to reveal the vibrant shade. I smiled and returned the lipstick to the shelf.

I had been sent out to get a list of first aid items for the girls, which was an errand Arnie had someone run for him often. He saw the girls as any other investment or collateral worth caring for, similar to taking a car in for scheduled maintenance. So here I was, filling a basket with vaginal creams, lubricants, topical solutions, band-aids, condoms, and a handful of prescriptions including painkillers and antibiotics, which a doctor Arnie was connected with had written up. He had more than one doctor he used in order to keep the flies away from his shit. He also had certain pharmacists in his pocket, which was another reason I was there. I stepped up to the counter and a man wearing an assistant pharmacist nametag acknowledged my presence.

"Can I help you sir?"

"Your name Masterson?"

"No. He's on his lunch."

"Did he go out for lunch or did he stay in for lunch?"

"Excuse me?"

"I'm a friend of his. Here to pay him a visit. Is he here or not?"

The assistant became uneasy. "He's in the back."

"Tell him Kendall is waiting for him."

"Um, okay hold on a minute."

The assistant disappeared towards the back room. I was alone in front of the prescription drop-off window. After about two minutes a man who was not the assistant came through the door. He was in his late forties and bald, with eyes that bulged from his head like a fish. He was a thin little man whose skin hung loosely from his body as though it had no elasticity at all. He spoke in a scared and nervous fashion.

"You people can't keep coming here. I could lose my job." He was whispering.

"Not my problem. Take it up with Arnie."

"Shush! Okay, okay keep it down will you?"

"I don't see how being inconspicuous is going to help at this point, do you?"

"Fine, okay. What do you want?"

I handed him Arnie's list.

He looked at it and his mouth opened. "All of this?"

"No, Arnie just wants some of it. The rest he wrote to practice his cursive."

"I can't. Someone will notice this much missing."

"Don't make me start from the beginning. If I leave here without it…"

He cut me short with wave of his hand. "Okay, please just stop talking."

I smiled. He took the sheet of paper and got to work. He worked quickly. I assumed he sent the assistant on break. It took him ten minutes to fill the various orders, which he handed me in three brown paper bags.

I had been doing a lot of these assignments for Arnie for some time now. The pay wasn't as good as the fights but I still got paid. Arnie also had me working directly with the girls and I often received non-monetary perks from those assignments. The work was small-time until a few weeks ago when Arnie and Pink had a meeting with me and asked me to start working on the itineraries for new container shipments of girls from overseas.

It was Pink's idea and Arnie went along with it. Arnie liked me, but it was Pink who had taken a real shine to me.

I was amazed at the intricate organization they had created and how far Arnie's business arms reached. He had his hands in everything but his bread and butter was the trading and trafficking of human beings.

The more work I did for them and the deeper I got into their syndicate, the more I was amazed at how much money one single human being would generate in revenue. One female was worth over a million dollars to Arnie and he was trading all over the world. He kept his head operations in Toronto though, due to Canada's visa exemption policies.

As clever as Arnie's whole racket was, his real genius was the creation of an online recruitment and advertising system, which was almost undetectable to law enforcement agencies, not just in Canada but worldwide. As far as operating, the system was very simple, yet extremely effective in both recruiting potential women and clients. Each client had to pass a screening process and answer a series of controlled psychological questions, which helped Arnie and his staff determine if the person was a real client or possibly law enforcement posing as a client. A final background check was also performed. All Arnie needed was a date of birth or social insurance number as well as a mailing address, and he could have an entire profile and dossier created on each client within 30 minutes.

The efficiency and accuracy of Arnie's operation, and his understanding of quality control and compliance was incredible. He could teach some of the top tier financial companies in the world a thing or two. For the first little while it was overwhelming and at times, I needed Pink to walk me through it.

Arnie had gone so far as to set up a series of failsafe protection systems to help mislead law enforcement, including systems that would flag IP addresses as RCMP or police stations. His safeguards were even accurate enough to flag remote sting operations. Arnie had been in business for almost 15 years and in all those years had never even received a slap on the wrist from the law. In fact, after a while I was convinced they didn't even know he existed.

It was around six in the evening when I boarded Dark Agnes, and Pink had been waiting for me. He was sitting in an outdoor lounge chair at the top of the gangplank. He waved me over to him.

"You get Arnie's stuff?"

I nodded.

"Good boy, give it here."

I handed him the bags. He took a cigarette from behind his ear and lit it, taking a long drag. He looked at me.

"What are you waiting for?"

"Arnie said you'd have something for me."

"He did, did he? Damn, you don't go easy, do you?"

He put the cigarette between his lips and shoved his hand into his jean pocket. He took out a wad of cash, unfurled three Robbies and handed them to me.

"Now go find a girl and leave me alone."

I put the money in my pocket and let him finish his cigarette in peace.

CHAPTER 17

Checkmate v. Stalemate

Each piece has a purpose, each with its own strength and weakness. The rook moves in horizontal lines and the bishop moves diagonally, but the knight makes an unorthodox move. Often described as an "L" shape movement on the board, the knight is the piece that most frequently catches an opponent off guard.

We had played four matches already, all of which Dietrich had won. In the fifth match, I managed to fork his rook and king with my last remaining knight. The loss of his rook evened the scoring.

Fourteen moves later, Dietrich managed a devastating blow and captured my knight with his bishop. I was left with only two pawns one of which could not move as it was blocked by one of Dietrich's pawns. Dietrich also had two pawns as well as his bishop. The advantage was his. Still, I gained position on his king with my pawn and had a clear line on the queening square. Dietrich was forced to capture the pawn, which removed any available square for my king to move to and the game was decided a stalemate.

"A draw. Well done, Kendall."

It was the closest I had come so far to a victory in our years of playing together.

"It was all I had left. I almost didn't even see it. I was going to move my King."

"With amateur players such as us, there is almost always a better move than our instinctual first glance at the board. It takes patience and observation, like in life."

"Maybe, but life doesn't always wait for you to make up your mind."

Dietrich smiled. His Form became exposed to me for the first time. I watched a white badger blink his eyes once, and then he was human again.

"Every time I see you, the cuts are deeper and the bruises are bigger."

He looked at me with genuine concern in his eyes. I didn't know what to say. I had become used to people staring at my mangled physical appearance that it didn't really affect me anymore.

"I just hope you know what you're doing."

It was nice to have someone show a little interest in me for once. I scratched an itch on the side of my nose and sat up in my chair. I watched as a new batch of people came through the arrival gate.

"It's not a fair place out there. I'm just trying my best to make do."

Dietrich didn't say anything and for a while there was a silence between us. We both watched families and loved

ones reunited after long periods apart and friends wel-
comed each other home.

"Maybe it's time to quit what you're doing."

I looked at Dietrich. I knew eventually he would say
something like this. It was

inevitable. He didn't know what I knew, hadn't seen
what I'd seen—the money, the women, all of it. He just
didn't know.

"I should be getting back to the city."

I stood up and tossed my empty coffee cup into the
trash.

"I was hoping we might play one more match."

"Can't."

"I see."

Dietrich folded the chessboard and put the pieces into
their respective containment slots.

"I'll walk out with you."

It was the first time he had offered this. Usually he was
in no hurry and liked to stay behind and watch a few more
sets of arrivals.

"You know, maybe it's time for you to start figuring out
what you really want for yourself."

"That so?"

"I guess what I'm trying to say is, we are all trying to
figure out what really matters, aren't we?"

"I know what matters."

"You do?"

"Most definitely."

We went through the revolving doors and stepped into
the warm afternoon sun.

CHAPTER 18

Friday –
Fight Night

I had poured myself a glass of water and then poured some milk in a bowl. I set it on the floor and Maneki came forward to lap it up with his tongue. He stopped for a moment and looked up at me.

"I appreciate this."

I nodded and watched the cat polish off the rest of the milk.

"Good?"

The cat's tongue licked at the corners of his mouth and then up over his nose a few times.

"That was delicious. I haven't had milk in years."

"Glad I could oblige."

"Thank you."

"So, you were saying?"

"Oh yes. Shrikun prefer darkness almost exclusively. In fact, you'll never see them in natural light."

"I see them in well-lit situations all the time."

"I am talking natural lighting, daylight. Shrikun find sunlight almost unbearable and would only try to claim a Form that they considered a monumental prize. You must understand though that this does not mean they are entirely comfortable with electricity, which as you know, is a naturally-occurring event. An electrical storm is terrifying for them. I know of two specific instances in my long history where Shrikun have been struck by lightning while trying to claim a Form and they simply disintegrated on the spot."

"So they can die."

"Be careful. That sounded dangerously close to a question and no they don't die, certainly not in the sense that you understand the word. Shrikun have three simple purposes which are to convert human Forms from white to grey and then to black, to witness death, and finally to acquire and collect Forms to use in clever and manipulative ways against humans. In the extremely rare chance one is destroyed, their Forms are disbursed evenly amongst remaining Shrikun in the nearest vicinity. As I've mentioned before, there are rules which are scientific in their exactitude."

"Those things friggin' stink, too."

"They are carriers of death. Death has a smell and it is not pleasant. Before you were endowed with these interesting visual aids, didn't you ever wonder why it was that you would sometimes catch the smell of death around you, that sickening distinct smell, but could see nothing? That is the smell of a Shrikun that is close; you just couldn't see it before. People always assume it is a dead pigeon or roadkill of some kind. Sometimes they are right and sometimes it is something more."

I looked up at the clock on the desk.

"It's time for me to go." I said.

"I know. Best of luck to you this evening." The cat skipped off the bottom steel of the portal doorway and then was gone.

I changed into some fighting trunks and threw on an undershirt. I sat down on the edge of the bed and reached underneath it for my boxing shoes and started lacing them up. I was ready to fight.

My first fight lasted three rounds, and I pummeled the guy in the third. He was an easy opponent and I would have knocked him silly in the first round, had Arnie and Pink not informed me that they required three rounds for reasons they did not find necessary to explain to me.

My second fight lasted seven rounds and I had trouble in the sixth. I misread my opponent and he landed a solid right. For a moment, I saw stars but managed to regain my composure just in time and avoided a powerful left hook intended to send me to the dirt. In the seventh, I concentrated on my footwork and out-danced the other guy. I had access to his torso and I worked him over real good until his body just gave out.

I didn't fight again for another hour and watched men rise and fall. There were faces of fighters I had fought before and there were lots of new faces too.

Rusty fought three fights as well and had crushed all three opponents. He hit one guy so hard in the side of the face that he crushed his Zygomatic arch into pieces. Rusty's fierce intimidation tactics gave him an obvious edge over his opponents. I had not yet witnessed a fighter that matched his raw ferocity.

When my name was called for my final fight I walked past Rusty, leaving the floor.

"One of these days Arnie's going to put us in here together," he said tauntingly.

"I doubt it."

"You're afraid of me, is that it?"

"Nope, you're a pussycat. I just know Arnie values money more than he does a grudge match and we make him a lot of money. Why would he want to cut that figure in half?"

Man and the weasel are the only two animals that kill for pleasure. History has shown that between the two, Man values human life less than the weasel. Our lineage is lengthy—the Filipino Massacre, East Timor, Cambodia, The Holocaust, the Crusades, anything on the African continent—to show we are creatures that have built civilization on foundations of blood.

I walked down the steps and faced my opponent. His skin was the blackest black I had ever seen and his eyes were bone-white. I never met a black fighter that lacked confidence in the ring. I guess that's what you get when nobody ever gives you a single thing for free your whole life. You get awfully good at taking what you need.

He looked at me and I met his gaze. I could tell he was a real fighter. It's something in the eyes, I'm sure I've said that before. He started to dance in place and threw a couple of air punches to get the blood going again. I did the same. There was no point in hiding what you had; any fighter that made it to the third fight had already seen what you could do earlier.

The bell rang and the shrill sound consumed every corner of the room. We started to dance. I moved in first, but he gave me no ground. His defense was solid and the harder I tried to land something the more I realized he was not like any of the other fighters I had faced. His footwork was too smooth, each punch calculated with pinpoint accuracy. He was a professional. Arnie had fished himself a ringer and decided to pit him against me.

I swallowed two straight jabs after I had managed to deflect a right hook. He was good and I hadn't even hit him yet. I tossed two soft lefts and followed with a right and then another left. None of them connected and he popped me with another left in the breadbasket.

I took two steps back and gave myself some distance. I needed a second or two to think and to find some sort of weakness or at least a hole of some kind in his tactics.

He moved in and threw two more straight jabs with his left but my defenses held firm. I finally caught him with a solid right, just under his nose and trickle of blood trailed slowly down onto his lips. He didn't show any emotion though; he was deep in the zone. I knew I wouldn't be able to use any shark tactics to goad him. I needed something though, because he was wearing me down.

He connected with a strong left cross. I shook it off and danced back to give myself distance again. He moved on in, just as he had last time. He charged in strong with stellar combinations. I managed to bob and weave through them and land a solid right, square in his left eye. He staggered back and shook his head. He tapped the side of his skull and shook his head some more.

I watched only for a split second and then I moved in. I had found my break. It wasn't a weakness or a hole. It was sheer luck. I landed two right jabs that connected just under his jaw. He didn't see them coming, he couldn't see. My earlier right cross had detached his retina.

He tried valiantly to score from his right side but I had determined earlier that he was a strong dominant left-hander. I had him.

I stayed tight and clean and took no chances. I went through the playbook and hit him with nothing but cream. He was truly a great fighter; even with the loss of one eye, he still managed to dance out of sticky combination. I was relentless in my pursuit though and eventually I caught him with a towering roundhouse right and he went down.

He got to his feet at a six count but was teetering. I came at him before he ever had a chance to get his bearings. I planted two left jabs on his cheekbone and then a right hook in the temple. He fell like a redwood and the referee counted him out cold.

I stood there, sucking and blowing wind. My chest was heaving and everything on me ached. I had a gash on the bridge of my nose and could taste the blood. I had taken a thorough pounding and somehow managed to come out of it yet again.

I whirled around and raised my arms to the crowd. The cacophony of the erupting cheers broke my inner silence. We had given them quite a show. I looked up at Arnie and Pink. Pink was smiling at me. Arnie on the other hand was not and disappeared from my view.

CHAPTER 19

Saturday – Date Night

I shouldn't have knocked on the door. I shouldn't have even been there. I heard the rattle of the door chain and the door opened. Whatever turmoil I was wrestling with inside of myself faded completely; I looked at her and I knew I was there because I needed to be.

"Hi." I smiled at her.

"Please come in."

Her dress was loose fitting but sophisticated and her lips were coloured a soft red, amplifying the blue in her eyes. I wanted to say something but I've never been a man of many words. I stared, as a primitive man like me would.

She smiled and didn't shy from my gaze. Her smile faded as she investigated the cut on the bridge of my nose. Her eyes wandered to the cut over my eye. She realized what she was doing and smiled back at me again.

"Are you hungry?"

"Yes."

"Should we go out?"

"I was thinking I might try cooking."

She burst out laughing and then regained her composure instantly when she realized I was serious.

"Are you a good cook?"

"I don't know. I've never done it before."

I made use of the ingredients she had and made a real mess in the kitchen. The food turned out to be more than edible, or at least Karen said it was. I was a poor judge of cuisine quality, though. I'd eat my own hand if I had to.

"Would you mind if I asked you something personal?"

"Go ahead." I braced myself, not really knowing what to expect.

She set her fork down on her plate and took a sip of wine. She brushed her hair away from her eyes. Every move, every gesture, was wonderful to observe.

"That night you helped me," she started.

"Right."

"Well, I don't know much about these things but I have never seen another person fight like that except in the movies."

"Is there a question somewhere in there?"

"Why do you always have…" She made a gesture to the cuts and bruising on my face.

"Oh. I'm a boxer."

"Can't you get hurt really badly doing that?"

I smiled at her. "You get used to superficial wounds."

"They look a little more than superficial. I don't know how people do that sort of thing. It's so dangerous."

"Want a lesson?"

"What do you mean?"

"Stand up and I'll show you." She looked nervous. "Trust me."

"Alright."

"Place your legs shoulder width apart and point your toes forward. Make eye contact with me." I came beside her and put my hands on her hips.

"Make two fists but don't squeeze them tight, stay loose. Keep them about a half a foot apart, settled just below your eyes so they don't hinder your vision of your opponent."

"Like this?"

"Exactly." She smiled. She was having fun with this.

"Now what I'm going to show you is the basic 'One-Two' combination."

"Okay, I'm ready."

"You look ready." I said smiling. "You're right-handed, correct?"

"I am."

"Okay. Now I'm going to hold my hands palm out at either side of my face. I want you to jab like this with your left and then follow it around like this with a right hook. Get it?"

"I think so."

"Okay, give it a go." She did it just as I had showed her.

"Perfect, but always remember to return your dukes right back to their defensive position to protect your face."

"Okay. Can I try it again?"

"As many times as you like."

After about 15 more tries she lowered her fists and was breathing heavy.

"That's a workout. Must take some real guts to keep going at it."

"Sometimes. A little luck helps too."

"I don't believe in luck."

"No?"

"No. I believe in fate."

I laughed jeeringly. "You mean God?"

"Why not?" She looked angry and I could see I had actually offended her.

"Just seems like nonsense."

"You don't believe in any kind of faith?"

"I've never given it much thought. To be honest, I actually do believe in God, I think. It's just that he and I haven't managed to come to some sort of understanding."

"How so?"

"It's complicated."

"It always is." She looked at me her expression softened. "I'm sorry, I shouldn't have…"

I cut her off. "Don't be. I started it. Why don't we grab our coats and go for a walk. It's a nice night and we can bring the wine with us."

"I'd like that."

As we walked beneath the glow of the sodium street lamps, I realized how nice normal could be. I had forgotten what it was like.

"What are you thinking?" She asked.

"That I like this."

"Me too." She looked at me with intensity in her eyes than made me feel naked. "I don't think I've ever seen you vulnerable before."

She stopped walking and leaned in to kiss me, first softly discovering my lips with an earnest tenderness, then more passionately. I pulled her close into my body and I could feel her heart beating against my chest. Then it ended. We said nothing and started walking again. I felt her hand fumble for mine and we locked our fingers together.

After the walk we sat on the steps leading up to the front doors of her condo lobby for a while, drinking from our travel cups.

"Would you like to come back inside?"

"I would but I have to get going."

"Oh?"

"I do." I offered her no further explanation. What could I say? What could I possibly tell her? I was already in way too deep.

"Will I see you again?"

"Work on that 'one-two' combo first and then we'll see," I said, smiling.

She started up the steps. I watched her. Then I did something out of character.

"Karen, I had a real nice time."

"So did I." She smiled and headed through the lobby doors.

I had no idea what I was doing. I was acting foolishly.

"I was just thinking the exact same thing."

I turned around and Lamia was sitting on the steps behind me. She was looking up at the moon.

"I thought you said you couldn't read my thoughts?"

"You don't have to be a mind-reader to pick up on what humans are thinking. You creatures are like an open book." She brushed a fallen leaf off her naked shoulder and looked at me. "So I guess you know why I'm here."

"To spoil my fun."

"Is that what we're calling it? I'd rather classify it as reckless, wouldn't you?"

"Yeah, maybe."

"You've never been the brightest star in the sky though, have you?"

"Go to hell!"

"I've been. Weather's not all it's cracked up to be."

"You must be so bored."

"Often." She yawned. "Anyway, I'll leave you be, Willie."

"Don't do me any favours."

"And here I thought I had."

I almost told her to go to hell and realized I had already said it. Again, like she knew my thoughts, the awful bitch laughed at me as she vanished into the night.

CHAPTER 20

Lights, Music, Reflection, a Party

You'd be surprised how much you can still take from a person who has nothing. The strobe lights started to flash intermittently and the people moved in unison to the thud of the bass line on the dance floor. I watched them switch from their Forms and back again, melding together in a combination of lights, sound, and sweat.

I sat and watched and drank. Unfortunately, there were no fights that night, as Arnie was away on business. He had gone alone, which meant he was into something big. I could have used the money I would have inevitably received, but my body needed to heal much more.

The flash of the strobe light shone directly into my face, momentarily blinding me. I lost sight of the dance floor and my thoughts traveled to another place and time. I thought of Prowler. When I was a boy, I had a terrier dog whose name was Prowl, although everyone called him Prowler. He was born the runt of the litter. Among his many ailments, he suffered from chronic ear infections that bothered him so much that he'd scratch his ears until they bled. The vet put him on steroids to help him recover, which over time caused Prowler to develop cataracts, a known side-effect of the drug.

Prowler's life became even more basic than the typical dog's life. His body and mind resorted to necessary coping mechanisms to deal with the physical pain and his loss of sight. He survived on food and my love for him. He would wait all day with his nose at the door waiting to catch my scent. His nose was the only thing left on him that worked the way it was supposed to. I hated seeing him like that and we eventually decided to have him put down.

I can still remember the look in his eyes as the needle went into his leg. He didn't want to die; although he had been in so much pain, he had lived with it so long that the pain had become all he knew. Hurting was as much a part of his life as I was, and he still had the will to live. I knew better though and said nothing as the vet pushed the plunger down the syringe and the translucent liquid flowed into Prowler's warm blood. I watched his eyes look right into mine and beg me to stop it from happening but I didn't. I loved him too much. As he slipped from this earth, I held his still body and cried into his matted fur.

"You thinking about the past?"

I blinked from a flash of bright lights and when my eyes opened again, Danika was standing in front of me.

"You shouldn't do that, you know."

"What's that?" I asked, smiling at her.

"Think about the past."

"I wasn't thinking of anything. Nothing but barbiturates floating around in here tonight kiddo." I tapped the side of my noggin with a knuckle.

She rolled her eyes at me in a childlike way.

"An old friend maybe, someone you can't talk to anymore?" she asked pryingly.

"I don't have any friends, Danika, you know that. Just irritations."

"Maybe a woman?"

"You're too smart for your own good." I put the tip of my forefinger between her eyebrows. "It's gonna get you in trouble one of these days."

"Come dance with me?"

"No."

"Please, one dance won't kill you."

"It might be the death of you." I said, although my joke didn't sway her determination. She only turned up the intensity in her eyes and I caved beneath them.

"Fine, one dance. You better not pull this crap when Arnie is around, kid."

She stopped walking and turned around to face me. I wondered if I might finally see her Form. Nothing happened though. She stood very still and said nothing at all. The coloured lights caught her young face, illuminating it.

"Don't call me kid. I gave up all childish things in this place long ago."

"If you could be somewhere right now, anywhere at all, where would you go? Where would you be?"

She was about to speak, her lips parted only slightly and then her eyes went vacant and I could feel her leave the room for a moment.

"Where would you go?" she asked.

"Wherever it is you just went to."

"One day maybe we will meet there, we'll be done with all of this." Her face was creased with sincerity.

"How would I find my way? I don't know where I'm going."

She laughed a little. "You'd feel your way, like a blind man or a child in the dark. The destination would speak to you like a song you've never heard before in reality but in your dreams it has played thousands of times." She trailed off and went silent again, in reflection.

"We would all be there and wait for the others to come and join us."

I watched as her cheeks flushed a little. I mistook the reaction for embarrassment about her moment of honest exposure, when in fact it was an incontrovertible belief in her own words.

She had such vulnerability and perfect raw humanity. I felt a terrible guilt for being a simple man, a fighter, a man of blood, and a creature of violence. She taught me something I would never forget; I'm not as tough as I thought I was.

We both didn't say much after that. In fact I don't remember us saying anything more at all. We just kept dancing and then drank ourselves into a coma. When we came out of it, I was getting punched in the tender flesh beneath my jaw and choking on my own blood, and Danika was being violently raped by Arnie.

CHAPTER 21

Giving in

I wasn't sure why I was at her door. Actually, that's a lie. I knew exactly why I was at her door. What I didn't understand was why I couldn't overcome the urge to be there. I had overcome everything else set in front of me, so why not this. I cursed as I knocked.

She smiled at me as she opened the door and then the smile turned to shock.

"Will, you're bleeding!"

I touched a scab beneath my eye. It was moist and the wound was oozing a little.

"It's nothing, really."

"Come in."

I did just that. I slipped off my shoes. Karen had run off towards the bathroom and returned with some tissue, bandages and peroxide.

"You really don't have to do this," I said.

I squinted as she dabbed the bandage wet with peroxide against the wound. I could hear it foam and fizz as the liquid did its job.

"This looks bad."

She remained in the same spot but leaned back a little to assess the wound after she had cleaned it.

"It looks worse than it is, believe me."

She did not. "Don't try to be tough with me. It looks like it is so painful."

"I never said it didn't hurt." I smiled at her and she softened up a little.

"What happened?"

"I got in a fight."

The words weren't a lie. Only their connotation was.

"You're impossible."

"You might be right."

She lowered her head. This wasn't going as I had hoped. She returned her eyes to mine. "What are you doing here?"

I wasn't expecting such a direct question. It caught me off guard. I ended up giving her more than I wanted to.

"I wanted to see you."

"Oh?"

She looked into my eyes and I realized it was much more than that.

"I needed to see you."

"Oh." She smiled softly at me.

"I should have called first."

She didn't say anything. She stood up, collected the first aid supplies and walked away. This had turned out to be a terrible idea. Then she yelled out from the bathroom.

"Care for a drink?"

"Yes!" Something else I needed.

I sat at her kitchen table and she took two glasses from the hutch.

"All I have is vodka."

"That'll do."

She set the bottle on the table and poured a shot in each glass. We chinked glasses and put back our shots simultaneously. I wiped my mouth and she grimaced in pain.

"I haven't had a straight shot since college and now I remember why."

I chuckled. "It gets easier by the third one."

She looked at me speculatively. "Does it?"

"Uh huh."

"Shall we have another then?"

I nodded and she poured.

"Here goes."

She raised her glass and again we sent back our shots. She winced again and I laughed.

"You're enjoying my plight?"

"I am." I realized I wasn't the one who was in control of the situation. I wanted her and I was sure she knew it.

"Third time's a charm, is it?"

I poured this time and I could feel her eyes all over me. "Have you had enough of this game?"

"Only if you have," I replied.

She didn't say anything. She got up from her chair and came over to me, putting

both hands on my chest, and leaned in and kissed me. It was a warm kiss that quickly became hot and powerful. I moved my hands to the small of her back and her long dark hair fell all around my face like swathes of silk. She threw her arms around my neck. "Take me to the bedroom."

I stood up with her in my arms and her legs wrapped around me.

"Which way?"

She was kissing my neck softly and pointed towards the stairs. We made it is as far as the middle of the hallway.

CHAPTER 22

Fire on the Water

I rolled over and landed in a beautiful mess of hair. It smelled wonderful and I breathed deeply. Karen's breathing was heavy and even; she was still deep asleep and I watched her, which brought me such comfort. I turned onto my back and stared at the ceiling for a while, I don't remember how long. I sat up and looked out the window. The moon was low and had cast dashes of silver ink on to the indigo of the lake's surface. The view was spectacular from Karen's condo.

"You shouldn't have done what you did, Willie."

"I know."

I turned and Lamia was standing in the doorway. She entered the room and took a seat on the chair in the far corner.

"You were right to leave her be years ago. The life you had then was complicated and now, today, things are even more difficult for you. Do you care for this woman?"

"I do."

"You can't have it both ways. You'll have to choose which is more important, the life you have or this woman. If you try for both, well you know what will happen."

"Do I?"

She looked at me with that smile, her exposed skin almost glowing in the darkness of the room.

"You do what you want then. Break noses and sleep with whores, then come over here for a taste of normalcy."

"Fuck you!"

"And your vocabulary, most impressive. She must love your sophistication, Willie."

I didn't respond to her jab. After all, she was right. I stood up and walked closer to the window. There was something burning on the water's surface. I squinted, trying to make out the tiny illumination. What was once very small suddenly burst into a large green flame on the water's surface. The flames stood out vibrantly against the water's dark surface. The fire looked controlled and contained in size.

"It's a Will-o'-the-wisp."

I turned and Lamia was gone. Maneki was sitting on the end of the bed. It was beginning to feel like Christmas Eve all of sudden. All I needed was a Shrikun in the room, some chains and a pair of slippers.

"Stupid name."

"I didn't name it." His tale was wagging and curling playfully behind him. "It signifies a death or more often, a death to come."

"Mine?"

"You'd think you'd have learned by now." The tabby shook its head with sincere disappointment. "Once you ask I can't tell you. Rules…"

"Are rules," I said, finishing the tabby's sentence. "Make an exception this time."

Maneki lowered his head for a moment. "I can't even if I wanted to. Once you ask, the information disappears, like it didn't even exist for me in the first place. I can't get it back."

I looked at Karen, who was still sleeping.

"Could it be her?"

"Maybe, I really don't know anymore."

I wrung my hands out in front of me in frustration. It was my own damn fault. My lack of patience had cost me the most vital of information. The cat stared at me for a moment, then leapt from the bed and started towards the door.

"Where are you going?"

It turned its head back towards me. Its eyes were heavy with what seemed to be sadness.

"I have nothing more to offer here at this time." Maneki continued through the door and was gone. I turned back to the window and looked out at the still-burning green flame on the water's surface. Then it suddenly vanished; there was not a trace that remained of its existence, no smoke, nothing. I found my pants and shirt and put them on.

"What are you doing?"

I turned around and Karen was sitting up in bed. Her chest was exposed and one arm hung languidly across her breasts. She looked warm and relaxed.

"I have to go."

Her expression changed and she subconsciously pulled the covers up over her exposed body.

"Really?"

"Yes."

"I wish you'd stay until the morning. I'll make breakfast."

"I can't."

She looked at me with speculation.

"Can't or won't?"

"Both."

"I missed something here. I didn't think this was just about you getting me into bed."

I realized there was no easy way out here, so I told her the truth.

"I'm not a good person, Karen. I'm part of something. The bruises and cuts, my knuckles... I fight men for money. I've killed men for money. I can't be with you. I thought maybe I could, but it would just be a lie."

"I don't believe you. That's not the person I've seen in you."

"I'm a master manipulator and you've been suckered. I wanted to see what it would be like to be with someone like you and now that I have, it's not worth it."

She didn't make a sound but tears fell freely from her eyes. I collected the rest of my things as she stared at me, almost stoically. I on the other hand was a coward. I looked away from her and left the room, leaving her behind with the pain that I had caused her. I was even enough of a bastard to think I had done her a favour.

CHAPTER 23

Her Story

I smelled coconut. I was on a lot of pills because almost everything on my body hurt. I took a pummeling but despite the pain, which there was a lot of, it's the parts that didn't hurt that worried me the most. The pain I understood, but it's a different story when something goes numb. I took the pills Arnie had at the afterparty. I didn't know what they were but after a while I didn't feel much anymore, anywhere. I didn't even feel the Latina broad on top of me who somehow managed to give me an erection, which told me I must have found her attractive before my vision transformed into striations of blurred colour and my ears filled with the bass of the nearby party. Her skin smelled of coconut lotion.

I fought two fights that night and was still undefeated, however, it is safe to say the last fight was a draw. I knocked him down, but he hit me harder and better. I was able to find a brief moment of weakness and I made good on it. It was obvious though that he was another trained fighter. It would appear that Arnie was finding a better crop of competitors. This one tried to mask his technique with that of a street thrower, but once a man gets tired he loses his control, and his real training shines through, or at least I figured that's almost always the case.

This guy fought with a calculating style and his footwork was too good. Street fighters have bad footwork but they make up for it with ferocity. I analyzed the fighter carefully. I visualized the ring and how he moved. The fighter came towards me and let loose a massive roundhouse that streaked towards my face. It was unstoppable.

I opened my eyes and at the foot of my bed, Maneki was sitting upright, looking at me. It was morning and the Latina was nowhere to be found. Had she ever really been there?

"How did you sleep?"

I frowned at him and said nothing.

"Don't be like that. I'm just here to check on you."

"I doubt that."

"Sadly, you're correct."

"Figured."

"Something's happening. There's a change and I've noticed Shrikun…"

"I'm not in the mood for any of this right now."

"I see. Well, William, you can't always get what you want."

The tabby tilted his head slightly to the left and I looked in the same direction. Danika was sitting on a chair in the corner of the room. She had a queer look on her face.

"Do you always talk to the cat like that?"

"What?" My mouth remained wide open.

"Talk like that, to the orange tabby cat."

"What cat?"

She sighed. "You don't fool me. The orange tabby that just strolled out of the room; do you always chit chat with him like you just did?"

I took a moment to collect myself. I was finding it hard to contain the impact of what she was saying. She continued on without an answer from me.

"He's my friend, too. Sometimes he sees me to sleep at night."

Suddenly the boat shook powerfully and we started to move. I looked back at Danika, who was stroking her hair in a childlike manner.

"Tell me something, Danika."

She looked up at me like I was going to say something more. "Like what? A story?"

I sat up in bed and pointed carelessly at the half-full water bottle on the night table. She handed it to me. I took a swig and wiped my mouth. "I mean, tell me anything at all. A story works. Just nothing with fairies, okay?"

She made a face at me then she fidgeted nervously in her chair. "I have a story for you."

I nodded and took another drink of water. I was so damn parched from the night before.

"Have you ever heard of a town called Sobinov?"

I shook my head.

"No one has really, but that is where I come from. It is in the Czech Republic. It is a very small place and one of great beauty. My parents own a farm there—pigs, cows. I have two brothers and an older sister. She is married and has two children of her own. I remember we used to have the most beautiful picnics in the fall. There was a quarry and a river we all used to swim in and then eat on the shore. My mother made Pavlova. Have you ever had this?"

I shook my head.

"It is wonderful." She stopped talking and looked down at the floor. When she continued speaking, her eyes remained lowered.

"I had a friend who was few years older than I. She was going with her parents to Paris for a week. They were flying from Prague. She asked if I wanted to come with her for the weekend to Prague and we could go dancing. I had never been to Prague either. I had never been out of Sobinov. Papa and I fought over it. I said some very nasty things and he gave in to me."

She looked back up at me.

"In Prague, my friend and I waited for her parents to fall asleep and then we snuck out into the night. We were turned away from three nightclubs before we managed to plead our way into the fourth. We danced all night and then my friend went to the bathroom and we lost each other. I looked everywhere and then a man offered to help me. I was so distraught and he was so nice and calm. He offered me a glass of water from the bar. I drank it. The next thing I remember, I was in a dark room with muffled voices."

I sat up. I hadn't realized I was listening so intently.

"Then a door opened and the room flooded with so much light that I could not see anything. I felt a prick in my arm and then I remember nothing more. When I woke again, I was in a boat container with twenty other girls. Some were very sick. We had very little water and food. The rest I am sure you know."

"No fairies," I said grimly.

"No, no fairies."

I finished my water and pulled the covers off me. I sat on the side of the bed.

"Should we have a little breakfast?"

She nodded and pulled her chair to the small table and joined me.

CHAPTER 24

A Gambit

"The rook is your only chance."

"You think so?"

"I know so. You've just lost your queen, you must capture the knight or you fall 16 points behind."

"I don't like to be told what to do."

I advanced my pawn. It was now just one move away from Dietrich's start line.

"Foolishness. Now I'll capture your pawn with my rook and you are now 17 points behind and only three moves from checkmate."

"You're wrong. It's only two moves until checkmate."

He looked over the board, carefully examining his two move-winning option.

"I think you are mistaken. There is only a victory in three moves that I can see."

"That's because you're looking at your options and not mine."

In sacrificing my queen I had taken his attention away from my minor pieces. In doing so, I advanced my pawn for sacrifice, which at the time was protected by my bishop and prevented his rook from taking the piece. Now that the pawn had been moved to an unprotected space, Dietrich advanced his rook one line forward to capture the pawn. This allowed me to advance the other pawn to A-8 that had been sitting so patiently in the A-7 position. I selected my queen as the piece to be returned to the board. It was check but not mate. He had to return the rook that had captured my pawn to its previous position, a move that only briefly stalled the inevitable. I slid the queen forward and captured the rook.

"Checkmate."

"A gambit! Well played. You had me so wrapped up in capturing your significant pieces I forgot about that damn pawn."

"It happens."

He slid back into his chair and looked around. I did the same. The airport was busy and we watched the crowds of people come and go. Dietrich reset the pieces on the board.

"Shall we play another?"

"I don't think so."

"Oh?"

I smiled at him. "Play like a champion and leave as one."

I took a sip of my coffee and watched a fresh batch of arrivals emerge from the sliding doors into the arms of their loved ones. I thought of the meeting that Arnie had called for that night and shook my head.

"Something wrong?"

"Maybe."

Dietrich put his hand on my shoulder.

"You can give this up. It's no life, you know?"

"No I can't. It's all I know."

"No, it's not."

Dietrich's eyes pierced into my soul and I saw him change to his Form.

"Should I quit what I'm good at? Work in a hardware store, pull a 9-to-5, pay taxes, become a contributing citizen after all this time?"

"I can see I'm not going to change your mind."

Then there was a silence between us for some time as we watched the tide of crowds come and go.

"Why a hardware store? Seems a little arbitrary."

"I don't know, I was spouting off. It was the first thing that came to mind!"

He knitted his eyebrows a little in confusion and then started to laugh. So did I. Dietrich laughed louder and harder and I joined him. People walking by turned to stare but neither of us cared, not even a little.

CHAPTER 25

May 29th 2006 –
Measuring Life

I saw an Amur Leopard once. I had a short-lived janitorial gig at the Toronto Zoo when the animal was brought in. Poachers had injured it. Cruel as that was, crueler still was the realization that the remainder of his time upon this earth would be behind cold, unforgiving steel columns, being watched by the creatures which were the very cause of his incarceration. We had the beast for a month. I went to see him every day when my shift ended.

When he moved, he was the noblest living thing I had ever seen. A king cloaked in the finest regal coat of speckles and a crown of ivory incisors as deadly as they were venerable. His body was sleek and lithe, every inch rippled with muscle. The real beauty though, the true source of his power, was in his eyes. He would look into my human eyes and knew he would always have one special thing that

I would never have, true freedom: to roam and answer to no one. No society, no government, no money, but only the most primal and instinctual responsibilities were his.

Sometimes I would watch the Leopard for hours. Often he wouldn't move and watch me in the same manner. It was a little game we played. He would survey me, size me up, try and figure out my intentions. Eventually the night would come and the beast would win the game by default. I could no longer see him in his tomb of shadows but he could see me and I know he watched for me, long after I had gone.

By 1990, around the time I worked at the zoo, I often overheard the zoologists talking about how there were only one hundred Amur Leopards remaining in the wild. They were endangered then. There are even fewer now, and they are likely to become extinct.

There is an incalculable amount of mosquitoes across the globe. Human beings crush them with ease between their thumb and forefingers with almost no thought at all. We don't have to hunt them and we don't covet their hides. We swat at them, spray them with pesticides, lure them into clever traps by the hundreds, from which there is no escape. Still they flourish because all they need is a little blood and water. The mosquito is crude and simple, while the Amur Leopard is beautiful and complex. The mosquito will survive the leopard. Humans are like mosquitoes; we take so much blood that we balloon grotesquely until we can no longer fly or worse, we pop and make a mess of everything.

We know it too; we just choose to ignore it. The really smart ones, I mean true geniuses, are often exploited for government means, building missiles of horrifying accuracy or writing useless computer code for the sake of a faceless corporate bottom line. The physically beautiful specimens are almost exclusively exploited when their minds are supple and malleable, ultimately leaving nothing but a beautiful brittle shell of what was once something that could have been a magnificent work of art.

The criminal, the man in control of this latter type of exploitation, the person who runs sex in this country, is Arnie, and every country has a man just like him.

They brought her in, three men dragging one woman on her back, howling and flailing across the floor. They let go of her arms and legs and she got herself onto her hands and knees. She was outnumbered eight to one. Nine if you count me. I watched her transform from the young woman I knew into the animal she needed to be. Her teeth were bared, muscles taught, body poised and ready, as she backed herself slowly to the wall. She looked at me for something, anything, but I had nothing I could give her.

The men laughed and Arnie stood there looking at her. She was afraid; her breathing was shallow and the blood had gone from her face. I knew Arnie would rough her up, maybe even give her a proper beating but she would fight him all the way through it.

The men in the room were either smirking at her like hyenas or mindlessly gawking as she recoiled defensively to the wall behind her. Arnie watched with great entertainment and then finally spoke.

"You know, there's nothing worse than a horse that won't run the race. The horn sounds, the gates open, but the damn thing just stands there with the jockey beating its ass."

The men all laughed at this and Arnie waved a hand and continued.

"Can't do anything for a horse like that."

He smiled and walked over to Danika, who had one hand braced against the back of the wall as though it was the only tangible thing in the whole world. Arnie smiled at her and put his index finger up in front of his lips.

"You see, some just won't be ridden no matter what." The smile he wore left his face.

"Some just can't be broken and some, well, they just won't be broken. That's the problem with human beings. Some, although very few, have a will that won't be tamed."

He looked Danika in the eyes when he said this and I noticed a faint shiver course through her.

Arnie's hand gently caressed Danika's cheek. She didn't flinch like I had expected her to. She didn't even blink and held his gaze firmly as he taunted her. He ran the back of his hand down the nape of her neck and then held it for a moment at the base of her clavicle. He continued to drag his hand over her right breast, reminding her of every time he had hit her, beat her, raped her. Still she gave him nothing. She was the strongest woman in the world at that moment and Arnie knew it. He took his hand away.

"I want you to know that I respect that about you."

Danika grit her teeth so fiercely, they might have been crushed into a fine powder and then spoke.

"You are very long-winded but ever so short where it counts. I wonder if it's still rape if you can't feel the prick?"

Her comment was a foul worm that had burrowed deep beneath his skin. No one else had noticed him falter. I did though, and he exposed his black jackal Form. It wasn't more than a moment before he regained complete composure. He reached down and took her small right hand in his. "I really do respect it, but I can't use it and I rather hate it."

His grip tightened and with his right hand, he took an open straight razor from his pocket and ran it across her forearm with medical precision and opened her ulnar artery. She looked down at the gaping wound pumping life from her body. She fell to her knees and tried to hold everything in that was spilling out.

Arnie crouched down on his haunches in front of her and mocked her with a false smile.

"It's better for you this way, trust me."

I watched in terror. My heart loosened from my chest cavity and fell into my stomach. I did not shout any disapproval; I didn't make a sound at all. I just stood there and watched her fall, hijacked by horror.

I was frozen for a time and then I formulated a plan, or what I decided was a plan of sorts. I took the beer bottle in my hand and emptied it on the floor at the feet of the man standing to the right of me. Then I took the bottle and broke it over the man's head. As his legs slowly gave out beneath him, I took the jagged neck of the bottle's remains still in my hand. I jabbed it deep into the neck of the other man standing to my left, removing the gun from the holster against his ribs when he instinctively brought his hands to his throat to try and remove the jutting glass from it.

I opened fire and killed the man standing in front of the shot meant for Arnie. Arnie dove and disappeared behind a couch for cover. I fired two more rounds at another man who had finally reacted to what was going on and was pulling his weapon free from its holster. He fell as two slugs burst his chest wide open.

I had managed to make it to Danika before I felt a bullet graze the right side of my waist and then sink into the wooden desk beside me. It was Arnie who had fired the shot. I turned and sent three more rounds in his direction that missed him and murdered the leather couch moonlighting as his savior.

I scooped Danika up into my arms and kicked open the cabin door as two more bullets zipped past my ears. I ran hard and noticed Danika's eyes were open. She looked at me and smiled. She was still alive.

I ran harder through the hallway and then through another set of swinging doors onto the catwalk. I could hear men shouting from behind me and then I heard shots go off around me. I turned quickly and fired a wild shot that did nothing. It was luck and nothing more that got me back onto solid ground as the Dark Agnes was still docked.

There wasn't much time to think and I knew within seconds there would be gunfire all around me if I didn't find cover. There was an alley across from the harbour and I could see an old broken down Chevy sitting at the end of it. I made for the alley and the cover of the vehicle with no plan of action after that.

I set Danika down on the ground and sat her up. Arnie and his men hadn't seen me go down the alley but they knew I wouldn't be able to go far with Danika in my arms. It wouldn't be long before they found us. I took the clip from the weapon and realized I had three rounds left.

"What's your name?" Danika asked, her voice almost inaudible.

I stopped fiddling with the gun and looked at her. She had stopped holding her arm and looked at me, the life fading from behind her eyes. I got angry because I knew what was coming and so did she.

"Put the pressure back on your arm Danika," I said sternly.

She smiled at me.

"Don't, don't do that! Put your hand back and keep pressure on it."

She continued to disobey me and reached out with what little strength was left in her and touched my hand.

"What's your name?"

I put the gun on the ground and put her small hand in mine. It was so cold.

"William, my name is William."

"Nice to meet you." She was smiling softly.

"I'm going to go now," she said finally and her eyes closed.

"Wait!" I pleaded.

Her eyes opened a little and then all the way. Around me, three Shrikun had appeared, anxiously awaiting her death.

"No! You won't have her! Not this one, I won't allow it."

"And they won't. Look."

It was Maneki. I caught a flash of Danika's white lynx Form for the first time. I looked for the Shrikun but they were gone. I looked back for Maneki and the damned tabby was gone as well.

Danika tried to smile at me but couldn't. I had only seconds. I leaned in and spoke into her ear so I knew she could hear me. When I was done, the left side of her mouth curled up a little in a final effort to make a smile and then she left like she said she was going to.

Three slugs thudded into the old metal of the Chevy and brought me back to reality. Another shattered the back windshield. I peeked around the side of the car and five men, including Arnie, were at the end of the alley waiting to see if I would respond. I fired another wild shot so they knew I still had a few rounds left.

I looked away from the action towards the other end of the alley as another round of shots fired my way. I stared at the huge chain link fence in front of me. It would probably take me about seven seconds to climb and clear the fence and get a few feet under me to be out of decent range from their shots. That seemed like a long time but what choice did I have. Despite our somewhat deserted location, I knew Arnie couldn't risk attracting the cops with this ongoing fire. After all, this was not America and these things are not exactly commonplace. The fence was my only real option. I had two rounds left and decided it was best to try and make them count. I stood up and aimed at the men and fired both rounds. I dropped one man with one shot and the other missed Arnie only slightly.

The men returned fire and a bullet shattered the driver's side window. Glass sprayed chaotically and shards bit into my left side. I had managed to lower the odds slightly by killing another man but had paid for it in the process.

I looked back at the fence. It was now or never. I sprung to my feet and jumped onto it and began to climb. I heard Arnie yell and the men fired at will. I couldn't stop now. They knew I had nothing left in the chamber of my weapon. I made it to the top of the fence and there were sharp intertwined pieces of metal that cut across my chest and thigh. I fell from the top about ten feet and landed painfully on my left side and partly on my back. I ignored the pain, got to my feet and ran with everything I had left. Bullets streaked by me but none hit their mark. I kept running and did not look back, not even to take one last glance at Danika. I just ran.

Had I looked back though, I might had seen a glowing white lynx kneeling steadfastly, its soft blue eyes watching my flight with earnest, and what looked like a smile across its jowls as each bullet failed to meet its mark. I would have seen the death of my first white. I would have seen what hope looked like. I didn't though. I just kept running.

CHAPTER 26

Haste and Prudence

I had no time for finesse, so I put a rock through the driver's side window. I unlocked the door, swept off the seat, found the rock and threw it away. I popped the trunk to see if I'd get lucky and find a tool worth using in the spare tire kit, and I did. I sat in the driver's seat and forced the casing free beneath the steering column. Within seconds, the engine was running. I put the car into first gear, released the clutch and was gone. I instinctively looked into the rear view to see if anyone was following me.

The cold night air felt soothing against my hot flesh. As it blew in through the smashed window, it dried the sweat all over my body. I had stolen a 1992 Toyota Tercel because people on the run steal old cars. Old cars are unsophisticated and easy to hotwire. People only steal a Benz in the movies.

My hastily made plan required two stops. The first was to go by Karen's. I hadn't figured out what I would tell her,

I just knew I needed to see her. When I finally arrived at her place, the front door had been forced open. The door hadn't been shattered or kicked in and I could see it was a professional job. I got a sick feeling in the pit of my stomach. I gently pushed the door open and crept through quietly, but once inside I knew I was already too late. Whatever had happened had happened a while ago.

There were obvious signs of struggle. Chairs had been overturned and there was glass everywhere. A knife was on the floor, but no blood. That was the only good sign. I did a complete walkthrough just in case, but she wasn't there. Someone had taken her. Arnie's letter on the counter confirmed my worst fears. He had known about Karen all along and after tonight's performance had decided to get his revenge on me in the worst possible way. He couldn't have gotten to her before me, which meant he had taken her before the meeting tonight. This also meant he had me followed and watched.

I grabbed an overturned chair and sat down. I had made a lot of mistakes. I leaned forward in the chair and put my face in my hands. I felt a massive weight of fatigue overcome me. I was weary, beaten, cut, bleeding, but worst of all I couldn't think because I was just so damn tired.

I knew I had some time. Karen was alive, I was sure of that because after Danika, Arnie would know I wouldn't come for a corpse. Arnie was also the kind of animal who liked to watch another man's pain and suffering, so he wouldn't do anything to Karen until I was there. I needed to use the little bit of time I had to check my wounds and get some rest, if I was going to be able to help anyone. There was only place I knew I could do that, a place even Arnie didn't know about. I was going home.

I looked at the clock on the stove, which read 4:47. It was almost dawn. I went to the window and carefully moved the drapes aside and peered out. The night's ink had choked the stars. I could tell it was going to rain hard.

I took one last look at the place that had become my last refuge of grace. I was wrong to have believed I could have something like this for myself. It was selfish of me to have ever come to this place and put Karen in danger. I would do whatever I could to get her back to her life no matter what the cost, but first I needed to rest and get a clear head.

I quickly wiped my prints clean and left Karen's condo as it was. I returned the chair to its overturned position. Outside, I tried to start the old Tercel again but the damn thing would not turn over. I pounded my fists into the steering wheel and cursed. I cased the parking lot for another option but there was none.

I checked my pockets to see if I had any cash. I found a crumpled twenty. I cursed again. A twenty wouldn't get me very far and who knows what I might need it for. I put the bill back in my pocket. I would have to press my luck and hitch a ride. I was already exhausted. For a moment, I thought about crashing on a park bench but I waved that idea off. It was too dangerous; I needed to get out of sight.

I needed to get rid of the Tercel as well. I put the car in neutral and put one hand on the steering wheel and the other on the frame of the broken window. I began to push. It only took a moment to wheel the car out of sight. I then wiped the car free of my fingerprints as well.

I looked up at the tumultuous sky. It was going to piss down any second. The air was cold and the sweat had dried on me in a bad way. I needed to get moving. It was a long way to my mother's place.

CHAPTER 27

May 30th 2006 -
Running on Fumes

I had devoured the apple my mother gave me. I was starving and it took the edge off.

My mother lived in Barrie. I walked to a nearby fuel station and used a payphone to call a cab. I hadn't been waiting long when the taxi pulled up. I got in and told the cabby the direction I was headed and he put the transmission into drive. Out the window, I watched the last of the houses slowly fade away until there was only countryside. I leaned forward and told the driver to pull over. I paid him with the last twenty bucks I had been saving and he drove off, kicking up dust behind him as he made his way down the dirt road.

I started walking. There were a few scattered fragments of clouds in the sky but they would soon evaporate as the morning sun burned them off. I threw the gnawed apple core away. I was standing in a field that was nothing but open space, except for one lone elm tree. It was 150 feet tall and the trunk about 20 feet in diameter. The tree was easily over 200 years old, in perfect health and was one of the most magnificent living things I had ever seen.

I picked up the spade shovel I had stolen from the farmhouse where the cab driver had let me off. I drove it into the earth beneath the tree and started to dig. I dug about two feet deep until I struck steel. I got down on my hands and knees and cleared the soil away from the object. I braced myself and pulled it free from the ground. I looked down at the small steel safe. I had purchased it years ago and lugged it all the way out here. It was my back-up plan, my safety net. I rotated the combination dial. I heard a soft click, turned the handle and the door swung open. I reached inside and took out a Smith and Wesson Sigma 9 mm and set it on the ground beside me. I reached back inside and took out five bundles of cash. I flicked through one of the bundles with my thumb and remembered there was two grand in each bundle. I reached back inside and took out the last item, a Kershaw flick knife. I pushed the release button on the handle and a 6-inch blade shot forth.

I took one bundle of money and folded the stack of hundred dollar bills into my pocket. I put the other four bundles of the money into a brown paper bag and wrote a short note on the outside of it with a black marker.

I picked up the Smith and Wesson and pulled the clip from the housing. It was full. I clamped it back into the pistol's handle and put it back in the safe. I closed the door and spun the combination dial. The weapon would be useless to me in this type of caper. The knife on the other hand was ideal. I picked up the flick knife and put it in my pocket.

I slid the safe back into the hole and took the shovel and buried it again. I patted the earth down and leaned the shovel against the tree. I followed its beautiful limbs with my eyes, all the way to the sky.

I started walking back towards the farmhouse with the filled paper bag and shovel. My stomach howled at me. I realized the apple had done the best it could and it was time I got something substantial in my stomach. I knew just the place.

When I finally got to the farmhouse I walked up the gravel driveway. I climbed the steps and laid the shovel beside the door and then I set the brown paper bag in front of the doorway. I turned and walked back down the steps. Moments later I was at the end of the driveway and then an hour later I was in a cab heading for the city.

That evening a man in his late sixties opened his porch door and stepped into the cool night air, with a pipe filled with fresh tobacco in his mouth and a book of matches in his hand. He kicked something over at his feet and looked down. He picked up a brown paper bag and read the words written in black marker across the front of it.

"For the use of the shovel."

CHAPTER 28

Ride the Rocket

"Is there a bottle in the house that someone would order if they were trying to impress a friend?"

"Yes sir, it is the 1988 Latour."

"Is there a bottle in the house that a man would order if he were trying to impress a woman?"

The waiter smiled almost imperceptibly.

"That sir would be the Château Mouton Rothschild 1982. It was considered a monumental year. The price of the bottle…"

I cut him off. "That so?"

He corrected himself. "Well sir, I might tell you that a patron once said it is the bottle you would order for your last night on earth."

I fished in my jean pocket and pulled out a bundle of pallid Robbie Bordens and handed them to the waiter.

"If there's not enough you let me know, if there's too much, keep it."

"Will do, sir."

The New York strip loin had been cooked medium rare to perfection. It would be in a place like this. The first morsel was just shy of nirvana. Whatever few steps to heaven were missing, the '82 Rothschild built with ease.

I rolled the wine over my tongue, allowing my taste buds to become accustomed to its subtleties. I decided the best thing to do at this time was to have myself an agreeable meal.

I sat in Bardi's Steakhouse after spending the day amongst the city's human traffic. If you've ever played 'Hide the Thimble' then you know the hardest place to find what you're looking for is in plain sight.

My meeting with Arnie wasn't until midnight, as his letter had instructed. What kind of person fawns over a $65.00 piece of flesh, swallows $900.00 worth of crushed grapes and then smokes $35.00 of Cuban tobacco while an innocent woman is in the hands of the devil? A man like me, that's who. Worry is a pitiful human condition and yields no positive results. Better to focus on primal human sensibilities, like a full stomach. A man thinks well on a full stomach.

"Mind if I join you?"

She was the last person I wanted to see right now.

"I'd give anything to wipe the ever-present smirk off your face."

"Anything?"

"Anything, you crazy bitch."

"Your soul?"

I said nothing. She had me again.

"Thought not. You act so tough, Willie." She dipped a finger in my wine glass and slid it between her lips. "I was in the Château when they were bottling this vintage."

"What do you want, Lamia?"

"No time for pleasantries, always business with you." She put the backside of her

slender hand over her mouth as she yawned. I hated this creature. "I know what you're up to, Willie."

"Do you?"

"Oh yes. You're going to pursue that tired platitude all men love so much. You're

off to play hero and rescue the damsel in distress. What a bore."

"It's my fault she's in trouble."

"Maybe, but no more yours than it is hers. She could have rejected your advances.

She wanted it as much as you did, maybe more, in fact."

"I don't expect a creature like you to understand."

"No need to be mean, Willie. All I'm saying is it's not all on you."

I put down my fork and knife. I took a sip of wine to try and clear the bile that

was shooting up my throat.

"Give me my supper, won't you?"

The grin left her face and a look that could almost be mistaken for benevolence

replaced it.

"A little advice then. I'd take the subway."

"I don't want your advice."

"Suit yourself. Don't waste the wine."

She got up and left the restaurant through the front door like a normal person would do. She also had a point. The subway was the best and most discreet route. I got up from the table, threw a few more Robbies down and walked out. Outside, I lit a Bolivar and started walking in the direction of the subway.

You can get lost in the sway and shift of the subway as it moves along. The train picks up speed and the platform runs away from you. Deep in the tunnels, the grey concrete races past as quickly as everyday life. I caught the train at St. Andrew, transferred at St. George and was now on my way to Jane station. From there, I'd walk. In the meantime, I sat and collected my thoughts. It was one of those rare occasions where I had the entire car to myself. It only lasted three stations though. A lone man got on at Spadina and sat down on the bench across from me as though it were the only seat left in the car. He smiled at me and I, for some inconceivable reason, smiled right back at him.

"Feels like you're off to war."

"Excuse me."

"Sorry for being bold. I can see you'd prefer your space. I can certainly appreciate that. I didn't mean to be rude or pry."

As he spoke, I caught a glimpse of his white wolverine Form. I had never seen a Form like that before. I leaned forward on the bench and sized him up.

"You've got an accent."

"I do?"

"Where you from?"

"America, but I'm Canadian."

"Been there a while?"

"I guess I have."

"What brings you up this way?"

"Business."

"Oh yeah, what kind?"

"Music."

I didn't care and the man could tell. I had a sudden compulsion to be direct. I felt something strange, like I had known this person in another life.

"What did you mean about going to war?"

"I'm sorry, I shouldn't have said anything. It's none of my business."

"Apology accepted, but humour me with an answer."

"You looked like you were weighed down with some heavy introspection. I know the feeling all too well."

"That so?"

"Yes."

"So what'd you do about it?"

"Found a woman." He didn't laugh or smile like it was a joke, but rather just stared at me intently. "You married?"

"No. Marriage wasn't in the cards. You?"

"Yes, recently actually."

"Kids?"

"A daughter and we just had a son, Jack."

I smiled at him. This was so far from anything I knew or would ever know and yet I felt a rapport of some sort with this man that was undeniable. I visually interrogated the man without restraint. I found nothing, not even a modicum of untrustworthy characteristics.

"If you are going to war, remember that the real enemy is the one you can't see."

"How so?"

"Fear."

I laughed a little inside at his bullshit, and played into it for the amusement.

"And how do you defeat fear?"

OF VIOLENCE AND CLICHÉ

"With a will stronger than that which inflicts the fear."

"If it's all the same, I'll stick with these." I held up my dukes.

The man looked at the two horribly scarred fists. They were battered and tired. He smiled a sad smile and his right hand subconsciously rubbed his left hand. It was brutally scarred and mangled. I hadn't noticed, having been so self-absorbed in my own thoughts.

The subway came to a stop and the automated voice announced High Park Station. The man started through the opened doors and then turned back around outside on the platform.

"Take care." He waved at me.

"Will do, um…"

"Oh sorry, my name's…" The subway doors closed before he could finish and the train rolled on.

I looked out the window beside me. In the tunnel, the concrete walls streaked by and suddenly gave way to a wide opening in the subway tunnel. I looked out into the void and an uncontrollable shudder riveted through my body. I thought I saw Shrikun enshrouded in darkness, although I couldn't be sure, as it seemed impossible. I could have sworn I saw hundreds of them, waiting.

CHAPTER 29

A Reprisal (Of Sorts)

The house was in ruin. Hell, the entire block was destitute. Even after all my years on the street, it amazed me that Third World neighbourhoods like this exist right here in this city. The windows were boarded up and there were blackened char stains from previous fires, most likely the results of an old meth lab.

I didn't see any easy entry points. I had a feeling they knew I was already there, so there was no real need in trying to be discrete. The front door was ajar, so I let myself in. Rusty was waiting on the other side with a 9 mm pointed in my general direction. He appeared to be alone.

"You always were weak," I said, and spat on the floor.

Rusty lowered his weapon and set it on a table. A faint smile broke across his face.

"Pound for pound and man to man?" he asked as he cracked his knuckles loudly.

"Suit yourself."

He smiled again and then exposed that black raccoon Form of his. Three Shrikun came from the kitchen, although they kept their distance and observed silently. Despite their stench, I did what I could to ignore them.

"You waiting for an award, or what?" I said, trying to antagonize him.

My tactic had worked and he came at me. He threw a hard right and I let it connect to some extent. In doing so, I lost my footing and we both fell to the floor. Rusty put a fist in my stomach but I was ready for it. It still hurt, though. I managed to get my hands around his throat, which is where I wanted them to be. He struggled for air and put a fist in the side of my neck, which made me lose my grip. He stole my idea and put his hands around my throat. The struggle on the floor continued. I was shocked that no one else came to his aid and then I realized this was what Rusty wanted. He wanted the opportunity to have me all to himself. He wanted to fight me, one on one.

As I thought about this, I struggled to stay alive and gasped for air. I saw something catch the light on the floor and I tried to reach for it. I didn't have a lot of time before I would start to lose consciousness. He had an iron grip and I felt my eyes watering from the pressure. By this time, the Shrikun had surrounded us and salivated as they watched our struggle. I edged my fingers along the floor until I finally felt the shiny object and I had it in my hand. I wrapped my fingers around it and then I drove Stentinowski's tooth and the silver hilt that it was attached to into Rusty's left eye. He released my throat and I sucked air greedily back into my lungs.

Rusty didn't make a sound despite the pain he was obviously suffering, which was unnerving to say the least. What happened next was even more unsettling. Rusty slowly pulled the silver shaft out of his eye and then threw it back to the floor. A single stream of blood ran slowly from the wound. We both got to our feet and he lunged at me, though I was able to reach into my pocket, concealing the flick knife in my hand. I quickly pushed the release button on the flick knife and plunged it into his Rusty's heart. He fell onto the floor and died mere seconds later, his cooling blood mixing with the other stains in the carpet.

Rusty reverted to his Form. The Shrikun looked down at the black raccoon Form of his and they began to fight amongst themselves. Each wanted it for their own and eventually one of them won.

I stood in horror at the idea of having to witness the terrifying act of a Shrikun devouring a Form, yet again. The experience was cut short however by a blunt pistol-whip. I didn't lose consciousness completely, but was mostly senseless as they carried me up the stairs. So much for any plans I had made.

I estimated my disorientation lasted about five minutes. I blinked my eyes hard and surveyed the room. Arnie was standing with his back to me, lighting a cigarette. I was tied to a steel chair that had been bolted to the ground. Beneath my chair, Arnie had placed a car battery and some cables with clamps on the ends.

Karen was sitting in the only other chair in the room. She was not bound and looked generally unharmed. She was clearly afraid though, and for good reason. But she was alive and this alone kept me going.

My chair was against a wall so I knew there was no one behind me. Arnie turned around and took a drag from his cigarette. He let the smoke out through his nose and then flicked the cigarette away, having barely smoked it.

"You know what I don't understand? Why a man like you would go to all that trouble for a dying, useless whore? Why is that? How does a man like you suddenly go soft like that? You, a man who has beaten other men to death, fucked whores to his heart's content and has grown up under the system just like the rest of us? I thought about this and I thought hard. Then it came to me. You knew the feisty little bitch, didn't you? Maybe she was a woman you used to poke? Nah. Someone you grew up with? A friend? No, I don't think so. You say you grew up here, in this city. You sound like the city. But what do we really know about you?"

"Do you want me to answer you or are you going to continue answering your own questions like some asshole?" There was no use trying to placate him at this point.

He laughed genuinely and then went cold. People like him can do that and switch from one temperament to another without hesitation.

"You were always sharp, Kendall. You can fight too, you really can. I liked you and what you could do with these!" He held up his fists and shook them.

"I respect these. So I gave you big jobs, the things you asked for and you repaid me with a bullet. Now I find out about this as well." He pointed at Karen without looking at her.

"I think about that feisty whore and this other bitch and something doesn't add up. I don't think I'll ever know the real truth."

"You might be right."

"I figured, but we'll still try. It saddens me, all of this."
He waved his arms in the air. "You betrayed me, you betrayed yourself, and for what? They are just women, my friend. They are ours to do with as we see fit. This is a man's world."

"Maybe so."

He came towards me and got down on his knees to fiddle with the car battery underneath my chair. I could hear the hum of power. I struggled a little to see if I could fight my way free, but I was bound and tied up well. Arnie wouldn't make that type of mistake. Still on his knees, he looked up at me with nothing more than simple complacency in his eyes.

"I take no joy in this. But I will enjoy myself with her, mark my words."

He tapped the nude ends of the clamps together and blue sparks burst from each.

"We are good to go." He touched the ends to my arms and I felt the white hot rush of electricity shoot into me. It lasted only a moment, but that moment felt like an hour. Steam left from my mouth as I exhaled. Karen was screaming at him to stop. She got up from her chair and started to come forward, and Arnie unsheathed his weapon and fired a warning round that just missed her. She fell back into her chair and cursed at him.

"A good start for all of us, don't you think?"

Again he set the clamps against my bare skin and I convulsed violently. I was sure another jolt would kill me. But I had to take that chance.

"Anything to say?"

"Turn it up. I find it cold in here."

"My kind of fighter. This will most likely be your last."

I don't remember much after that. I remember the initial contact and I do remember Karen screaming but nothing more. When I came to my senses, Arnie was standing over me, smiling and I was drooling profusely. I started to say something but nothing came out of my mouth except blood.

"Looks like you're bleeding quite badly. That's a first."

I didn't respond to his taunts. I raised my head and tried to keep my eyes from rolling back into my sockets.

"You want to know the truth?" I was whispering.

Arnie came a little closer to me so he could hear me better. "I do. But I don't think you'll tell me."

"Yes I will. I have no reason not to. Not at this point." I spit out another mouthful of gooey blood.

Arnie got down on his haunches so his face was next to mine.

"I don't want her to hear me."

Arnie looked over his shoulder at Karen, who I could tell was ready to fight to the death. That was the only gift I could give her, the one I wanted to give her in case things didn't work out.

Arnie turned back to face me and shuffled in closer. I started to speak in a whisper that made the words I was saying almost imperceptible. Arnie came closer still. I leaned forward and whispered in his ear.

"I liked both of them, a lot. That's the only reason."

Arnie smiled and his jugular bulged on his neck's surface. I took the razor blade I had concealed in my mouth, the one from the medicine cabinet I had taken from my mother's house and slid it forward on my tongue. The blade had ravaged my gums during my convulsions. I clamped my front teeth down hard on the blunt end, jerked my neck fiercely and raked the razor's edge over his pulsing and pro-truding vein.

Arnie's eyes widened as I did it. Blood spurted from his neck onto my chest. He stumbled backward and fell. I watched him writhe on the floor, pressing his palm against the irreparable damage.

Vengeful thoughts flooded my mind and in that mo-ment, I hated this man more than anyone has ever hated anything. Then as suddenly as my volatile emotions had swelled within me, they were gone. I felt nothing. I was empty. I just watched him squirm a little more until he was still and dead. I spit the razorblade out of my mouth and tried to catch it in my hand but it was slick with blood and slipped to the floor.

"Karen!" She was still looking at Arnie's lifeless body on the floor and the almost perfect halo of blood around his head.

"Come on, Karen! You have to get the razorblade and cut these zip ties around me. Hurry."

She came over to me and reached down to pick the blade up off the floor. She looked at me and froze.

"It's okay. Come on, you have to cut me free quickly."

She managed to cut through the first restraint and set my right hand free. I took the blade and cut myself loose from the other bonds. She helped me over to Arnie's corpse and I reached underneath him and pulled out his .45. I looked her squarely in the eyes in an attempt to refocus the both of us.

"Stay behind me and…" I wasn't able to finish as a bul-let went through my shoulder. The weapon I was holding came free from my hand and slid towards the far wall. I turned around and another slug went into my gut. I fell. It was over. I pressed one hand softly on the gaping wound in my stomach and removed it to see the crimson stain that covered my palm. It may seem ridiculous, but it was as if I needed verification that what I though had happened actually happened in reality.

Pink was standing in front of me, holding a smoking beretta.

"I told Arnie it wasn't worth it, that he should just kill you and be done with it. He was sure there was something more going on with you and he needed to know. Fuckin' broads, always get under our skin, don't they?"

I couldn't move. My shoulder and my arm were useless, and I was bleeding out from my stomach wound. I had managed to prop myself up on my good arm, but I couldn't hold that for long. I didn't have a lot of time left, maybe only minutes.

"I don't understand."

"Really?" asked Pink, mockingly.

I scowled at him. He came over to me and crouched down to my level, which was Arnie's big mistake. Sadly, I didn't have any aces left up my sleeve.

"This may surprise you, but I don't like to see a man suffer when there's no need for him to do so."

He raised his gun level with my eyes. I knew what was coming and I was ready for it. I had never been an evil man but as I said before, I was never one of the good ones. I had done what I could. I closed my eyes and heard the crack of the gun firing. I opened my eyes instinctively at the sound, and realized that Karen had fired a single round at Pink but missed. He spun around and trained his weapon on her. With my final bit of strength, I swung my arms around his legs to get him off balance, and managed to jostle the weapon from Pink's hand just as it fired. Although the shot missed Karen's torso, the bullet found another mark and knocked the pistol she was holding from her hand.

Pink got to his feet and ran towards her before she could scoop up the weapon. He grabbed her by her throat and slammed her violently against the wall. As he began to choke her, he took his free hand and started to slide it under her dress. She tried to wriggle free but he only tightened his grip on her.

"I want his last moments on this earth to be spent watching what I am going to do to you. It is going to be depraved and ever so violent."

Her eyes started to roll back in her head from lack of oxygen and then she remembered the razorblade I had handed back to her. She managed to find some strength to rake the blade across Pink's cheek. It cut him deeply and blood ran from the wound down his face. I could see his grip loosen and he instinctively removed his hand from beneath her dress to touch his face. With the little fresh air that had suddenly filled her lungs, she drove her knee into his crotch. A guttural sound escaped his lips and he doubled over. She took two handfuls of his hair and drove his face into the wall. I heard a cracking sound and Pink stumbled onto the floor. Blood was flowing freely from his nose, which was now horribly broken. He looked up at her, with rage.

"Fucking bitch. I'm going to really hurt you."

Karen showed no sign of fear. I watched in amazement as she got into a fighters stance and put up her fists just like I'd shown her. Pink spat blood and then started to laugh at her, mockingly.

"You're kidding, right?"

Karen didn't say a word and held her position.

Pink looked down at the gun. It was between them. He started to move towards it and Karen advanced on him.

"Fine, I'll go a round with you." Pink moved in on her. Karen waited for him and then threw a left jab and then a right jab. Both connected. It was a perfect "One-Two" combination. Pink staggered backwards, more from shock than from any pain.

"Fuck!" She had goaded him, which was to her advantage. People make big mistakes when they lead in with rage. Pink made this mistake, and went after her with his full force. She held firm and jabbed him in his broken snout and then hit him hard with a beautiful right hook. He stumbled to his knees, with his hands covering his face.

Karen ran forward and picked up the weapon as Pink started to crawl away from her in a pathetic effort to escape. She fired two rounds; the first missed its mark and the second buried itself into his groin. He wailed in pain. Karen attempted to shoot him again, but the next shot barely grazed his ear.

Pink continued to drag himself in my direction, moaning pathetically as he did. She continued to fire unwieldy rounds until finally, a slug penetrated the right side of his chest with a dull thud. Still, she kept firing even though there were no bullets left and the weapon made an empty clicking sound. He stopped moving, his breathing slow and laboured. She lowered the weapon and stared down at him in disgust.

Pink looked over at me, his mouth agape. "I knew..." Whatever else he was going to say got strangled in his throat.

I realized that this man was the reason for so much pain and suffering. He had fooled many people, including me, into thinking that Arnie was the man behind it all. I watched him choke and gasp for precious air that would no longer come.

"While we're waiting here, let me tell you a little story, Pink."

Pinks eyes widened only slightly as his life began to run away from him. He tried to move but his strength had left him.

"Dark Agnes de Chastillon was a woman that men tried to enslave but she rebelled, killed her captors, and won her freedom. She would later become a warrior and helped bring down an entire empire, or so the story goes."

Pink coughed and little spots of blood smattered along his lips in an effort to talk.

"Only fiction..." He tried to laugh, but only continued to cough.

"Is it though?" I looked up at Karen as I said it. Pink's eyes followed mine and the smile on his dying face was replaced with one of humiliation as the gurgling sound of his last breath escaped his lungs.

A Shrikun emerged from behind me and walked towards its two prizes. I had never seen one exercise such patience before. I watched in horror as it acquired Arnie's black jackal Form and then with its giant gaping maw swallowed Pink's black tiger Form. Their fetid stink froze my heart. Witnessing a Shrikun perform this terrifying act almost caused me to feel pity for its victims, these truly evil men. Almost, but not quite.

Karen was still holding the weapon and pointing it towards Pink, clearly suffering from shock.

"He's dead and the weapon is empty. Karen," I called to her gently.

She looked at me, blankly.

"Karen, he's dead. Go grab the other gun. It's likely someone else will be showing up here right away."

She brought it over to me, silently.

"We need to get you some shooting lessons."

She didn't laugh at my ill-timed joke, nor did I. She stood over me, my unlikely protector. Against my will, I lost consciousness.

CHAPTER 30

April Fool's Day

My head was resting in gathers of royal blue silk. I was in Lamia's lap and she was stroking my hair. Maneki was there too, sitting by my side silently. Lamia gazed down at me with heavy eyes.

"I'm going to miss our mutual antagonism, Willie."

I looked up at her, a little bewildered. I searched the room for Shrikun but none could be seen. I wondered if you couldn't see them when they were coming for you, but to be honest, I didn't want to find out.

I tried to move and winced in pain. I looked back into Lamia's face but it was now Karen who was holding me in her arms. She looked me up and down. Her eyes welled up.

"You're dying."

"I am."

"Can I talk you out of it?" She attempted a smile. For a moment, she shifted into her Form and I looked into the scared dark eyes of a white deer. My eyelids had become so heavy and they started to close.

"Please, don't," she whispered. Had there been anyone else in the room, they would not have heard it.

I realized I had forgotten one final item and I pried my eyes open as best I could. I fished into my pocket and placed what I was looking for into her hand.

"What's this?"

I hadn't the strength to explain it. Everything she needed to know was in her hand, anyway. She buried her face in mine and I could feel the warmth of her skin against my cheek. In that moment, the pain from my wounds left me. I could hear her sobs grow fainter until I couldn't hear them anymore.

CHAPTER 31

Revelations and the Like

You'd like what you do in life to matter. It could be an arrogant and self-important human concept, and it probably is. But regardless of motivation, it is a notion that is as inescapable as fate.

It was a Tuesday like any other when I was hit for the first time. Donald Sterling hit me hard enough to make it count and I remember the salty taste of blood on my tongue. I was 11.

Eight years later, the World Boxing Association sanctioned a fight with the existing welterweight champion of the world, Oscar De La Hoya. It was a title match and his opponent's name was William Jackson. That's me.

I had been fighting my whole life on the streets and I fought my way into a world championship match. I didn't show up at the weigh-in and that was the end of that. But I'll tell you right now that Mr. De La Hoya was no match for me. He was pretty though, for a pugilist. I would have been the first Canadian welterweight champion of the world since Lou Brouillard in 1932. But I'm blowing old smoke, and old smoke is stale by nature.

The item I had placed in Karen's hand was a key. The key had a piece of masking tape wrapped around it, with a name on one side and an address on the other. The address was for a place she was sure she had never been before, and she was right.

The police had questioned Karen for hours. When they had their fill and let her leave, she went home to find two Canadian Security Intelligence Service agents waiting for her at her door. She had expected a police guard but not CSIS. The agents introduced themselves as Thompson and Dietrich. They asked their questions too but at this point Karen had no answers for them, not yet anyway.

She had taken a cab to the address on the key and ended up at Tiny's Gym. With predictable irony, Tiny wasn't tiny at all. He was a big man with a big heart who had spent years training me as a fighter. I would have turned out a hell of a lot worse if it wasn't for his thoughtful influence.

Tiny told Karen that I was one of the greatest young welterweight boxers in the world, and that I could've been a champ. He told her I had been married and that my wife was my world. He explained that my wife, Catherine, had disappeared two months after we had found out that she was pregnant for the first time. She was found in a storage container on a boat bound for Prague, at which time her body had been expired for more than three weeks. My wife had died carrying my unborn daughter. We would have named her Grace.

Tiny choked on his words but continued through, telling Karen my story. Tiny knew that one day someone would come to see him about me, but he wasn't expecting it to be another woman. He knew I wouldn't be coming around anymore, but he knew I had done what I had to do.

After my wife's disappearance, a CSIS agent named Dietrich had come to see me about her abduction and death. Dietrich had offered me an opportunity. He needed someone who could fight, but not just any fighter, someone who could infiltrate Arnie's syndicate. I agreed to help and CSIS falsified my death so that I no longer existed. The only people aware of my past life were Tiny and agent Dietrich. For years I had been working under deep cover, clawing my way into Arnie's world and working for the likes of Loudon the Louse and other losers just like him. You cannot imagine my sense of relief combined with the urge to vomit when I sat down that first time years ago at Gen Go Chow, and watched Arnie slurp down those detestable noodles. I had finally made it inside the lion's den and I would spend every moment thereafter planning to burn it down. I could've put a bullet into Arnie's brain many times over and trust me when I say I came close to doing so a few times. But that would've only been a band-aid. Someone else would have taken his place. I needed to bring the whole organization down so other women like my wife and Danika would never have to live a life in slavery again. For Danika, I was able to let her know that her death was not in vain. When I whispered into her ear as she was slipping from this world, I let her know of my years of undercover work. I told her I would see Arnie's organization and others like it fall, even if it cost me everything, including my own life. It was a promise I kept.

Tiny took Karen to the locker where I used to hang up my gloves. She used the key I had given her to unlock it. Inside, she found some old pictures of me with my wife and it brought fresh tears to her eyes. But it was on the backside of the pictures where she found what I had sent her there to find; names, dates, times, patterns, an entire schematic to a worldwide network of human trafficking. My chess meetings with Dietrich at the airport were in fact information-sharing sessions, and not even Dietrich realized just how important the information I had collected was until it was later analyzed.

An entire international operation would be brought to its knees over the course of the next two years, supported by the data I had collected and the joint efforts of various governments and Interpol. Some of those arrested went to prison and others ended up with worse. Karen found twelve years of my work in that locker and put it in the hands of Dietrich, who moved the pieces on the board to checkmate.

Under Dietrich's leadership, 42 women were discovered on the Dark Agnes vessel. After lengthy investigations and miles of international red tape, all but two of the young women were reunited with their families. Despite this small victory, these women had their innocence corrupted in such a way that even on their best days, they still struggled to find a will to live.

I'm no hero. I am nothing more than a man who made a life out of falling down and finding a way back to his feet every time. I am an actor who has said and done things that I can never take back, because I needed others to believe. The only one I couldn't fool was Danika, and it was Karen that fate baited me with, testing my commitment to staying in character and playing the part.

The night falls without fail upon us all. We die and we don't come back. I could tell you what I know about the other side of it all. I could tell you there's a really nice place waiting for us that lies too far outside the reaches of anyone's imagination to even contemplate. Or, I could tell you that there is nothing to hope for at all and that when it's over, there is nothing left. But none of that really matters. What matters is whether you decide to put up your dukes.

La Rotonde

Pavlova and French roast

Out of the cold

M C Joudrey, was born in Sydney, Cape Breton. He studied graphic design and animation at Red River College in Winnipeg, though abandoned his studies for a time to travel the world as a professional inline skater. His collection of short stories entitled Charleswood Road was nominated for a Manitoba Book Award (John Hirsch Award). He and his wife currently reside in Winnipeg.